"HAVE YOU LOST YOUR MIND, *MS. WELLBOURNE*?" Jack gripped her by the arm and hauled her to a private table at the back of the room. "Just how naive are you, anyway? Don't you know that big bad boys like Bones eat uptown ladies like you for breakfast?"

Eden's chin went up defensively. "I'm still here, aren't I? And all in one piece, I might add, no thanks to you."

"That grateful for my help, are you? Face the facts, Ed. You'd be in serious trouble by now if I hadn't stepped in to protect you."

"Protect me? Ha! You were *pawing* me, and enjoying it just a little too much. You might've tried something more appropriate!"

"Fine." Jack laughed softly. "Next time I want to make my mark on you in a rowdy, redneck bar, I'll kiss you instead."

The scent of him enveloped her, assaulting her senses like a cloud of something dark and intimate, heavy with steaming male sexuality. Sexual, that's what his smell was. If she knew how to bottle it, she'd be rich beyond her wildest dreams.

WHAT ARE *LOVESWEPT* ROMANCES?

They are stories of true romance and touching emotion. We believe those two very important ingredients are constants in our highly sensual and very believable stories in the LOVE-SWEPT line. Our goal is to give you, the reader, stories of consistently high quality that may sometimes make you laugh, sometimes make you cry, but are always fresh and creative and contain many delightful surprises within their pages.

Most romance fans read an enormous number of books. Those they truly love, they keep. Others may be traded with friends and soon forgotten. We hope that each LOVESWEPT romance will be a treasure—a "keeper." We will always try to publish

LOVE STORIES YOU'LL NEVER FORGET
BY AUTHORS YOU'LL ALWAYS REMEMBER

The Editors

A SCENT OF EDEN

CYNTHIA POWELL

BANTAM BOOKS
NEW YORK · TORONTO · LONDON · SYDNEY · AUCKLAND

A SCENT OF EDEN

A Bantam Book / August 1998

ISBN 0-553-44670-3

Published simultaneously in the United States and Canada

Bantam Books are published by Bantam Books, a division of Bantam Doubleday Dell Publishing Group, Inc. Its trademark, consisting of the words "Bantam Books" and the portrayal of a rooster, is Registered in U.S. Patent and Trademark Office and in other countries. Marca Registrada. Bantam Books, 1540 Broadway, New York, New York 10036.

PRINTED IN THE UNITED STATES OF AMERICA

OPM 10 9 8 7 6 5 4 3 2 1

ONE

"Your wedding is only three weeks away, Eden, and if everything falls into place, it's going to be beautiful. There's just one small thing that seems to be missing. The groom," Hope said.

Eden Wellbourne glanced across the sparkling, scent-filled expanse of her family's Winter Park perfume shop and winced at the look of concern she read in her older sister's eyes. Hope was sincerely worried about Armand's uncharacteristic lateness, she realized with a sharp twinge of guilt. As maid of honor for Eden's wedding, Hope had already spent countless hours planning and preparing for the big day, making sure that everything would be perfect, right down to the last detail. In fact, her sister had so much to look after already, Eden didn't want to burden her with any fears of her own.

Armand's unexplained travel delay, for instance. Her fiancé was seriously late in returning from a scheduled business trip. Nearly three days overdue from an excursion that should have been routine.

"I'm sure he'll show up soon," Eden said confidently, attempting to reassure herself as much as Hope. In an effort to keep busy, she reached for the well-worn feather duster and proceeded to dust the long, warm-hued, wooden showcase of shelves where row upon row of gleaming glass bottles were displayed. "He's probably just a few days behind schedule and hasn't had a chance to phone," she added encouragingly. "I doubt Armand even realizes how late he really is. Don't forget, he's a chemist. The absentminded-professor type."

"Uh-huh," Hope murmured skeptically. "So was Dr. Jekyll. And he had a habit of disappearing too. Under some very strange circumstances."

Eden paused to brush a strand of smooth chocolate hair from her forehead with neatly manicured fingertips. What was Hope hinting at? That Armand was more than merely late?

But the steady, stable scientist she was engaged to could hardly be compared to the schizophrenic Dr. Jekyll. Dr. Armand Guillon, head research chemist for and heir to the House of Guillon, the renowned French perfume company, wasn't the least bit likely to turn into an evil Mr. Hyde. In fact, he was the most considerate, dependable man she'd ever met.

From Eden's first day of work in the Guillon scent labs, when she'd been fresh out of a Paris perfume school, Armand had been her mentor and friend. He'd taken her under his experienced wing, encouraged her, taught her to channel her skill into something useful. He understood her unusual talent as no one else had. He'd shown her how to see her extraordinary sense of smell as a gift, rather than the burden it had been for much of her life.

The new scent they'd created together was the culmination of everything she'd learned from him. In fact, he'd been en route to personally select the flower crops for that very same fragrance before he'd been somehow waylaid.

"It really *isn't* like him not to call," she admitted. "In fact, his reliability is one of the things that made me fall for him in the first place. He's nothing like Dad, you know. He's a man I can really count on."

Hope didn't speak. In fact, her sister had no need to say a word about their common family history.

Eden swallowed back the lump that rose to her own throat at the mutual, heartsickening memory. In spite of the seven-year age difference between Hope and herself, their dad's desertion was a wound the two of them still shared. Eden had been no more than a toddler when her attorney father had done the unforgivable deed and run off with his implant-enhanced office assistant, an embarrassingly young and overendowed woman their mother scathingly referred to as Saline Sally. But even though Eden could barely remember the subsequent divorce of her parents, the repercussions had been long and lasting.

Their mom had never recovered from the bitter blow. In the final decree Katherine Wellbourne had lost her husband, her home, and her pride. The perfume shop she opened paid most of the bills, but the struggle had been more emotional than financial. The comedown from charity hostess to charity case had literally killed her.

Pulse Points was passed on to her daughters when she died, but the small business wasn't the only thing Hope and Eden had inherited. Their father, too, had made his own contribution to their upbringing. Instead of the child support he'd been ordered to pay, he'd given his two girls a well-founded wariness of men.

"So what should I do?" Eden finally asked, thinking out loud. "Go to the police? I'm not even sure Armand has been overdue long enough for them to file a missing-persons report. Besides, he's not an official U.S. citizen. Would they even be willing to look for him?"

"Maybe not," Hope said, pulling a small scrap of paper from the file drawer just beneath the cash register. "But I have the name here of someone who would. A private investigator," she explained, dropping the neatly scribbled note onto Eden's outstretched hand.

"An investigator?" she asked in surprise, casting a quick, doubtful glance at the unfamiliar name and address. "How do you know this guy's any good?"

"I've asked around," her sister confessed. "This one specializes in missing persons. He's supposed to be the best in the business."

"Jack Rafferty," she said, reading out loud. "He's really legit, huh?"

"A near perfect track record, according to my sources. Go ahead," Hope urged. "Why not give him a try?"

Why not, indeed? Eden reasoned. What harm could it cause to at least go and see this Rafferty guy? She was already missing one perfectly good fiancé. What more did she have to lose?

"Your dog is dying, Mr. Rafferty. There's nothing else I can do for him."

Jack Rafferty felt the words lance through him, as cold and sharply clinical as the stainless steel exam table where Wolf lay, panting shallowly. This was it, then. After fifteen years of faithful service and friendship, Wolf was finally leaving him. Not even the costliest, most state-of-the-art animal clinic in Orlando could save the old dog's life. Jack put a callused hand out, stroking the grizzled mutt firmly behind one enormous, furred ear. Wolf's tail wagged weakly in response.

"Help him die, then, Doc," Jack ground out. "Can't you at least do that?"

Dr. Gallamore, fresh out of some expensive East Coast vet school and looking young enough to still be carded at the corner bar, flipped briefly through the final pages of Wolf's medical chart, then glanced up at Jack with a hesitant frown. "There is still the matter of your account with us, Mr. Rafferty." His appraising, businesslike glance seemed to take in every disreputable detail of Jack's clothing, from the blue jeans, shredded with wear, to the tattered, once-white T-shirt, now filthy with mud and reeking of wet dog hair. "Your balance, as it stands, is more than thirty days overdue. . . ."

Cold, hard cash. *That* was what the man was worried about? The fact that he'd let his account slide since Wolf had been sick and they'd both been unable to work? Jack resisted the urge to wrap his bare hands around the vet's greedy throat and throttle him hard. "You'll get your money, Doc. All of it. As soon as you take care of my dog."

Wisely refraining from pushing the subject any further, Dr. Gallamore made a scribbled notation on the last page of Wolf's chart, and shut it with a finality that wrenched Jack's gut. "That's it, then, Mr. Rafferty. I'm sorry we couldn't do more, but fifteen years is a long life for a dog. The euthanasia process will be merciful and painless. Please settle your bill with Ms. Crumley on your way out."

Still stroking Wolf's ear, Jack pointedly ignored the

hand that the vet stretched toward him. "I'm sorry too," Jack said softly, "but you're not going to be rid of me that easily. There's no way in hell I'm leaving without my dog."

"Trust me," Dr. Gallamore told him bluntly. "You don't want to be here at the end. Most people prefer not to stay."

"I don't trust anyone," Jack said quietly. "Except Wolf. And if you think I'm going to desert him now, you're an even bigger bozo than I thought you were."

The vet's narrow shoulders rose indignantly. "Now look here, Mr. Rafferty, I have a waiting room full of clients out there. *Paying* clients, I might add. I don't have to stand here and be insulted in my own clinic."

"No," Jack agreed, his tone deceptively polite, "All you have to do is make the end easy for my friend here and do it now."

Flustered, Gallamore shot an impatient glance at his watch. "I can't possibly get to it for another hour."

Grabbing a handful of the vet's lab coat collar, Jack jerked the astonished man's head up until their eyes were level. "*Now,*" he said, his voice a cold, implacable whisper. "Put my dog out of his pain."

Stunned by Jack's swift reaction, Dr. Gallamore began to babble. "I—I doubt he's in any serious pain. A slight feeling of discomfort is far more likely. His breathing is labored, but respiratory failure in these cases is usually slow and gradual."

"Discomfort, eh?" Jack repeated softly, taking the man's designer tie between his fingers and gradually tightening the knot. "Labored breathing? Slow respiratory failure? Maybe you'd like to see how it feels for yourself."

A strangled "No" was the veterinarian's barely audible response. "That won't be necessary," he choked hoarsely, as Jack slowly loosened his hold on him. "I'll do as you ask. I can see you feel very strongly about your dog."

"Very perceptive of you, Doc," Jack said. "Now, let's get on with it. . . ."

Five minutes later Wolf lay dead in his arms.

Without another word to the pea-hearted young vet, he carried Wolf out the clinic door, laid his lifeless body carefully across the front seat of his pickup, and headed for Lake Jesup and the houseboat he called home. He would bury Wolf there, along the sandy, palm-strewn shores and marshlands where the dog had loved to run on days they weren't working. He would bury his friend, his tracking partner, and the only living thing he loved.

The only living thing he had ever loved besides *her*.

Along with Wolf's body he would bury his final hope of ever finding her again.

By the time the grave was deep enough, a storm had rolled in across the central Florida sky, turning the swollen white clouds into melting black mountains, as jagged and wide as the hole in Jack's heart. He welcomed the whipping wind, the pelting rain, and the lightning as he covered Wolf's body with soft, moist earth. The downpour washed over him, mixed with the salty drops of sweat from his forehead, and ran in stinging rivulets past his eyes, a bitter, burning substitute for the tears he could not shed.

Jack Rafferty, the toughest, most tenacious tracker in the state, was incapable of crying. The man who had found more than a hundred missing persons, both dead and alive, had never wept for the one person he himself had lost. Nor did he weep for Wolf now.

He returned to his houseboat instead and poured

himself a stiff shot of whiskey on ice, dispassionately deciding it was too damn bad Doc Gallamore hadn't put him out of his misery as well. One easy injection, he thought, and it would have all been over. One little prick would have put a final period on the past fifteen years of pain.

Death, for him, might have been the easy way out, but now more than ever he had to find the guts to go on living. He had to remember the motto he'd played in his head for so long, his mantra, the mission statement that had sustained him through his grueling, sometimes grisly profession as a human body hunter: *An unhappy ending is better than no ending at all.*

Jack had helped so many families find the closure they needed; he had to keep going long enough to do the same favor for himself. He needed to find the ending to his own miserable story.

Tipping the glass back, he downed the shot in a single swallow, silently admitting there was just one small problem with that brilliant idea. He wasn't any closer to cracking the case than he had been fifteen years before. In fact, he had only one thing left to rely on. Himself.

Which was exactly what worried him the most . . .

When Eden finally reached the secluded shore along Lake Jesup Lane, she fervently wished she'd let her fingers do the walking and phoned ahead for an appointment instead of driving directly to the address that Hope had given her. For heaven's sake, there wasn't even a building standing where the PI's office should be, just an oversized houseboat floating in the waves that lapped the water's edge. She was tempted to turn the car around and head straight back for Winter Park without stopping, but on second glance she noticed a dark set of numbers boldly spray-painted across the swaying front door.

Three eleven. It was definitely the right place, but what legitimate investigator would set up shop out there, in the middle of nowhere? The closest house was a quarter of a mile down the dirt road she'd just driven and there wasn't anything resembling a real business anywhere in sight.

Still, she'd come this far. And she did have her dog with her for protection. Weighing in at barely three pounds, Babette wasn't terrifying by anyone's standards, but what the tiny teacup poodle lacked in size, she made up for in fierceness and loyalty. She had never been known to bite anyone, not even at the Guillon lab where she'd been caged the first year of her life until Eden had come along and abolished all company animal testing. Since the day Eden had adopted her, Babette's bark had been better than a personal alarm.

Eden shouldered her large tote purse in which the dog lay sleeping, and gingerly made her way across the sandy, overgrown stretch of yard that led to the investigator's front porch. "Anyone home?" she called out, knocking firmly on the houseboat door.

"Damnation!" was the gruff male response. Then, "Get lost, whoever you are. The check's in the mail. Take a hike."

"A hike," Eden grumbled loudly, "is exactly what I had to take to get out here in the first place. I'm looking for Jack Rafferty. Any idea where I can find him?"

"Yeah," the voice laughed roughly as the door flew open with a swift, booted kick. "In hell. He lives there."

Eden instinctively took a step back, blinking in

speechless shock at the man who stood before her. All six dirt-caked, disreputable, overwhelming feet of him. From the coarse stubble smattered darkly across the hard angles of his lower face and jaw, to the disheveled waves of sunlit hair, and the jungle-green eyes that were flashing at her in open annoyance, the guy didn't look exactly ready to receive company. In fact, the irritated expression that swept boldly across his suntanned face communicated his clear displeasure in no uncertain terms. The stranger definitely wanted to be rid of her.

Which, at first glance, was just fine with Eden. Because it wasn't just the man's overtly crude appearance that sent her senses reeling. It was his raw, overpowering odor. Eden's well-trained nose detected traces of wet dog, sweat, and fresh earth, but beneath those unexpected top notes was a base of something musky, male, and unrefined. Involuntarily she put a hand to her face to block out the disturbing scent.

"What's the matter, Princess?" the stranger demanded. "Smell a little game for a sweet thing like you, do I? Haven't you ever been this close to a man before?"

Horrified at her own unintentional rudeness, Eden dropped her hand back to her side. This stranger's blunt incivility was no excuse for her own. But there was no easy way to explain her unique, often troublesome talent to a man she'd never met. At times like this, having an exquisite nose could also be exquisitely embarrassing.

"I—I'm sorry," she managed to say awkwardly. "You just . . . surprised me."

"Ditto, darling," the stranger shot back. "But I thought I told you to leave."

Eden felt her temper begin to rise by several degrees. "Fine, mister. In fact, there's nothing I'd like better. So just tell me where I can find Jack Rafferty and I'll be on my way."

"Who wants to know?"

"Eden Wellbourne," she said reluctantly. "I need to interview Mr. Rafferty for a job."

"Tough luck, Princess," he told her. "I'm Rafferty. And the interview's already over." Jack felt a fleeting moment of remorse as he watched the look of sudden disappointment flash across Ms. Wellbourne's face. He was being rough on her, he realized, but it really didn't matter what the woman's problem was, he was in no shape to help her.

"*You're* Rafferty?" she said. "A licensed PI?"

"Oh, I'm licensed all right," Jack admitted. But to do what, he wasn't sure anymore. Without Wolf his tracking style was seriously compromised. And even if he did decide to take a case without the help of his late partner, it wasn't going to be Ms. Wellbourne's. "But I doubt I'm the man to do your job. I only take hopeless assignments. Hard-luck cases. And lady, you don't look like you've had a day of that in your life."

She put her hands on her hips, blinking up at him defiantly. "I don't see how you could possibly know that, or anything else about me, Mr. Rafferty, since we've never even met before."

Jack leaned back against the doorjamb, hooking his thumbs in the belt loops of his blue jeans as he studied the woman in front of him with a long, appraising look. No, he'd definitely never met her before, but one glance was enough to tell him all he needed to know. *High class* were the first words that came to mind. Yeah, Eden Wellbourne was cultured, a fine pearl, perfect and creamy, with her suit of buffed silk and her pale skin polished smooth to the touch. No doubt the lady had class and lots of it.

But there was something at odds with her stylish exterior that hinted at a core of pure sensuality. The woman hid race-car curves beneath her suit. Her satin hair was a few shades deeper than dark chocolate, and her large eyes glowed like flame-warmed cognac at the bottom of a brandy snifter.

The woman wasn't just well-bred. She was dangerous. And Jack didn't want a damn thing to do with her.

"I know enough," he said bluntly. "If the Winter Park license plates hadn't given you away, the uptown accent would have. There's only one thing I'm not sure about. What is it you need an investigator for?"

She folded her arms across her chest and shot him a glare cool enough to freeze fire.

"I—I had no idea I was so easy to read."

Easy? Jack wondered. No, there wasn't a thing about her that was easy. She was more the complicated, high-maintenance kind of woman. The kind who would want a serious commitment from a man or nothing at all.

Definitely not his type.

Jack preferred his women friendly and willing. And if they wanted a physical connection beyond friendship—well, that was just fine by him. Physicality brought its own kind of comfort and release. As for any further involvement, he simply wasn't capable of feeling the depth of emotion required for a serious relationship. Hell, he didn't *want* to feel it.

"Sorry, Princess," he told her, "but it's pretty clear you're a luxury few men can afford."

"Am I supposed to take that as a compliment?" she asked, defensively squaring her shoulders, "or an insult?"

"Take it as a hint to get back in your car and get a move on. You don't belong in this neck of the woods."

"That's it?" she asked, her voice softly shocked. "You're not even interested in hearing my case?"

Oh, he was interested all right, but not necessarily in her case. Which was exactly why it would be best for both of them to send Ms. Wellbourne on her way.

"Very perceptive of you, Princess."

"Stop calling me that! No one calls me that."

Jack glanced curiously at the understated diamond ring that was gleaming subtly against the third finger of her hand. "Not even the man you're going to marry?" he asked pointedly. "Seems kind of a shame."

She cast a quick look down at the simple, half-carat stone that Armand had presented her the day he'd proposed. Nothing else could have reminded her so quickly exactly why she was here. And why it was necessary to endure Jack Rafferty's unnerving, very unbusinesslike behavior for just a little while longer. No matter how disturbing the PI was to be around, he still might have the know-how she needed to solve her present problem.

Not that he'd exhibited any extraordinary stroke of genius so far. It didn't take a brain surgeon to read license plates, or pick up on the accent she'd acquired over the last few years living in France, or even to realize that an engagement ring worn on her left hand likely meant that she was engaged. But there was an uncanny kind of intuition he'd exhibited that told her he saw more than he was saying.

Besides, Hope *had* told her he was good at his job, and if her overprotective older sister had done the research, Eden knew Rafferty had to be better than he looked.

"The man who gave me this," she responded calmly,

holding up her hand, "is precisely the reason I'm here. My fiancé is missing, Mr. Rafferty. I was hoping you could help me find him."

She watched him bring a hand up to stroke the five o'clock shadow across his chin and was struck by unexpected contrasts. His wrist, she realized, was nearly twice the diameter of her own, with enough brute force in the thick cords and tendons to break bones in two with a single twist. But the fingers against his face were surprisingly lean and flexible, supple in spite of their obvious strength.

"Look, lady," he said, his voice heavy with frustration, "I'm not in the business of shattering hopes. Hell, if it wasn't for hope . . . well, let's just say I know it's not an easy thing to live with. Or without."

Her eyebrows rose at yet another surprising discovery about the hard-core, hard-to-read PI. He seemed to understand what she was going through. From years of work experience? she wondered. Or was he speaking from a more personal point of view?

"Then you'll consider taking my case?"

"Fact is, I'm also not in the business of tracking down cold-footed fiancés and forcing them to face the altar."

"Armand," she said indignantly, "does *not* have a case of cold feet."

"Uh-huh. Pretty sure of that, are you?

"Sure of *him*." She proceeded to relate the entire story. How she had flown ahead from France, returning to her hometown to finalize the wedding plans. How Armand had been required to make a few business stops before their preplanned rendezvous. No one, she concluded, had seen him since his visit to the orange groves. He simply hadn't shown up.

Jack shrugged, leaning back against the door again with the lazy, easygoing confidence of a man who had just solved her case for her. "I wouldn't sweat it, if there's no sign of foul play, sweet. If your boyfriend's as true as you tell me he is, he'll probably show up sooner or later. Then the two of you can kiss and make up."

"But we didn't fight!" she insisted in frustration. "Armand and I *never* fight. Our relationship isn't like that. It's based on mutual respect, not passionate arguing and unbridled physical apologies."

"Now *that* is a crying shame." He looked her over again, slowly, with his liquid green gaze traveling up and down the length of her in apparent approval. "In fact, it's a downright disgrace. No passion at all, Princess?"

Eden flushed hotly. "Excuse me?"

"I'd say it's poor Herman you should be making excuses for, Princess. Are you sure you want him back?"

"It's *Armand*," she said, striving to maintain her temper.

"Herman, Armand. Same name, different languages."

"*You* know French?" she asked, disbelieving.

"No, darlin', but it's my business to know names. And people."

"Armand is fluent in three languages."

"Must be a brilliant man," Jack speculated.

"A genius."

"Naturally. At chemistry, isn't that what you said, sweet?"

"Exactly," she assured him stubbornly. "Chemistry."

"Uh-huh."

Eden's flush deepened, along with her anger. It was impossible to mistake what Jack Rafferty was insinuating—that her fiancé might be brilliant in some areas of science, but sadly lacking in others. Chemistry, biology, it didn't matter what he called it, she knew what the exasperating investigator meant.

The fact that he was right about the relationship between herself and Armand certainly didn't make the accurate observations any easier to swallow.

How had he known, anyway? It was positively appalling how quickly this rough-talking stranger had assessed the single weakness in her romance—the lack of physical satisfaction. It wasn't poor Herman who was missing out on the sensual rewards of their committed relationship. It was Eden herself.

Since the first day of their engagement Armand had made gentle, tender love to her several times. He'd made her feel warm and wanted. He just hadn't made her climax.

Of course, Eden had never faulted him. How could she blame her fiancé when she knew herself to be the cause? She simply wasn't capable of physical fulfillment.

Armand, fortunately, didn't seem to mind too much. And Eden had consoled herself with the thought that sex was only a small part of marriage. Passion, thank goodness, wasn't so important if you really cared for someone.

But just when she was consoling herself with that eminently practical, completely reassuring thought, Jack Rafferty did something that suddenly stripped every ounce of her self-comfort away. He touched her.

"Don't look so sad, Princess," he said, reaching out with those long, sensual fingers of his to stroke her lightly across her cheek. "I was only trying to make a point. I didn't mean to hit a nerve."

Eden felt that single touch from his fingertips all the

way down to her toes. The sensation was so sudden, so electrifying, she stood rooted to the spot, her breath temporarily suspended in her throat as charges exploded somewhere deep in her stomach. He'd hit a nerve all right, she realized. He'd struck several dozen of them.

Before she had a chance to catch her breath or her bearings, Babette unexpectedly popped her head out of her purse and began to bark ferociously at the stranger.

"What in blazes . . . ?" Jack exclaimed, startled.

"Hush, Babette," Eden said, soothing the little dog with the sound of her voice. "It's okay, honey. Yes, I know, you were just defending me."

Rafferty did a double take as he stared down at the trembling creature. "As if that little thing could stop me," he said, laughing.

"Babette isn't a thing," Eden explained indignantly. "She's a poodle. And a highly intelligent one at that."

He shot another doubtful look at the pent-up animal. "Intelligent or not, I'd still say she's a mighty poor excuse for a dog."

Babette began to bark again, as if she understood perfectly what the giant stranger was saying.

Eden smiled. "I told you she was smart."

"Smart, maybe," Rafferty admitted, "but pretty much on the puny side. Better not let her down or the gators might get wind of her."

"Gators?" Eden asked, glancing uneasily around.

"Gators," he repeated firmly. "The lake's full of them. One bite and your mini-critter there could wind up as a tasty morsel."

Eden wasn't certain if he was telling her the truth or if this was simply some new tactic designed to frighten her away, but she wasn't about to take any chances and let Babette wind up as an alligator's hors d'oeuvre.

"Down," she told the poodle firmly, and was gratified to see her well-trained pet disappear inside the purse again and safely out of sight.

"At least she's obedient. Which is more than I can say for you, Ms. Wellbourne."

"Another compliment?" she asked sweetly. "How kind."

"Another warning, woman. It's time to be on your way."

He was starting to turn his back on her, summarily dismissing her with a single wave of his callused hand. She watched in simmering silence as he swung himself around on those long, booted, blue-jean-clad legs and strolled away from the houseboat, striding slowly into the sunset. He was *leaving*, just like that!

Eden wasn't sure whether to be sorry that the encounter was finally over, or relieved. She made her way back to the car, deciding to be grateful. What did she need with him, anyway? Luckily, the cell phone on the console rang before she had a chance to fully consider the question.

"Hope? Is that you?" Her sister's voice on the other end of the line was so distressed, Eden barely recognized it. "Has something happened?"

"It's the shop," Hope said, half out of breath. "It's been broken into."

"Are you okay? Were you there?"

"No, thank goodness. It happened fifteen minutes after I'd closed up for the evening. They shattered the window, made a mess of the front room. Rummaged through the back." Her voice caught. "Eden," she groaned, "it's a wreck."

Eden frowned as a shiver of suspicion ran through her. What would burglars be looking for in the back room of Pulse Points? The only items of any value were kept up front. The cash drawer, the bottles. It didn't make any sense for them to search anywhere else. Unless . . .

"Hope," she said, "as long as you're safe, we can deal with the mess. Now, just take a deep breath and tell me the rest. I need the details to be sure what to do next."

TWO

Five minutes later Eden hung up the phone. The stakes in her search had just been raised by the disturbing development back at the shop. It was no longer simply important that she enlist Jack Rafferty's help. It was imperative.

She pulled the car around and headed back down the dirt road, searching for any sign of the vanishing PI. Where had he taken off to? Half a mile or so later she had her answer.

Lizard's Lounge. She might've guessed the guy was headed for the nearest bar, and this one was exactly the kind she'd expect for him to hang out in.

Run-down, rough, ramshackle. The words didn't begin to do Lizard's fine establishment justice. The scent of stale beer wafted out through the open windows, along with the permeating aromas of hard liquor, old leather, and male perspiration. The slow strains of a wailing country-western song blared from the jukebox as loud oaths and deep masculine laughter competed for sheer decibel space. Happy hour, apparently, was in full swing.

Summoning her intestinal fortitude, Eden exited the safety of the car again and warily made her way up to the tavern door. Almost as an afterthought, she gave a quick tug on the band of her engagement ring and pulled it off, popping it safely into her purse. Lizard's didn't look like a very safe place to be flashing diamond rings around. With a final warning to Babette to keep a low profile, she turned the squeaking, protesting doorknob and pushed her way inside. Her senses roiled momentarily as she was blinded by the darkness and the full impact of the place hit her.

She blinked into the hazy, smoke-filled room, uneasily aware that the noise level had just dropped off significantly. When her eyes began adjusting to the weaker light, she started to understand why. All conversation in the joint had come to an end, along with the tune on the jukebox. Dead silence prevailed as all eyes in the bar focused back on her.

Male eyes, Eden observed, swallowing hard. No wonder she'd attracted so much attention. Except for a solitary, harassed-looking barmaid, she was the only woman in the place!

Worse, the men were ogling her as if she were the last pint of beer at the bottom of a keg. Men who gave new meaning to the term "party animals." Bikers in black leather, hoodlums, rowdies, and roadies were all a part of the questionable clientele that patronized Lizard's Lounge. Judging by the scores of empty beer bottles and the bone-dry remnants of scattered shot glasses, it looked as if they'd all been patronizing for a pretty long time.

"Hey, Lizard!" one of the party-harders called out, pointing thickly at Eden. "Is it ladies' night or something?"

If there were any holdouts in the room who hadn't been ogling her before, that question all but guaranteed they were gawking now.

"Naw," one of the good old boys in the back row answered before Lizard himself had a chance to respond. "Can't be. Chicks don't like to hang out here. And if they do, they sure ain't ladies!"

A raucous chorus of laughter echoed loudly around the room.

"She must be the evening's entertainment, then!" another man yelled enthusiastically. "I hope she can dance. Do you dance, lady?" he shouted to Eden, his speech slightly slurred.

"Don't matter, man!" a huge, bald-headed biker shot back from his ringside seat at the bar. "I think I'm in love with her anyway!"

An alarming series of whoops and whistles and catcalls followed this endearing declaration, sending premonitory shudders up Eden's spine. The biker looked absurdly proud of himself, and the debauched, male-bonding exhibition of pack behavior by his buddies gave him all the encouragement he needed to come forward. Hauling his slightly swaying Mack-truck frame off the barstool, he made his way purposefully toward her.

From a distance, Eden decided, he didn't look bad. He looked horrifying.

His head alone was the size of an inhabitable planet, and she could swear the floor shook when he walked. Still, she was determined to stand her ground, no matter what her persistent suitor decided to do. Showing fear in this sort of situation could only make it worse.

But then she got a good look at her newfound biker beau up close. A skull-shaped tattoo adorned the general area where his hair had once been. A brown leather vest, stained heavily with sweat, covered most of his shirtless torso. Unfortunately, it didn't hide all of it. The protruding beer belly, quavering and furry, was like a living thing unto itself. In an effort to tear her eyes away from the awe-inspiring sight, Eden tried to focus on the man's face instead and found herself staring at a shiny gold nose ring.

So much, she reasoned, for standing her ground. There was a lot to be said for the simple act of running for one's life. The biker was only a couple of feet away from her, and his greasy, sausage-sized fingers were beginning to grope their way toward her. But just as she began to wonder if she would ever make it out of Lizard's in one piece, a familiar form stepped in front of her, blocking her enormous admirer's path.

Jack Rafferty.

Eden let out a quick, shaky sigh, resisting the urge to fling her arms around his rock-hard chest and sob with heartfelt gratitude.

She wondered, with some concern, what he was going to do next.

To her surprise, Jack didn't flex a single, well-developed muscle at the other man. He wrapped one of his lean, tightly corded arms around her instead, pulled her incredibly close, then stretched his free hand around and gave her bottom a playful, possessive pat.

She turned a stunned face toward him, shocked into temporary silence.

The biker, too, stopped dead in his tracks. "This one yours, Rafferty?"

Eden struggled to find her voice again. "Just what do you think you're—"

If the look on Jack's face hadn't been enough to

render her speechless again, another bold tweak to her backside did the trick.

No one, in fact, could fail to notice the intimate, clearly proprietary way he was touching her. Especially not Mr. Skull-Headed Biker. But instead of knocking Jack instantly out of the way or challenging him to a fight, the cowardly giant started swearing in frustration.

Jack waited until the final epithet had died away. "Sorry, Bones," he apologized politely. "She came here for me. Didn't you, Ed?" he asked, treating her to a sexy, heart-stopping grin.

"Ed?" she repeated, incensed.

"Aw, man, Rafferty," Bones complained bitterly. "It just ain't fair. You get all the women."

One of the interested onlookers that had gathered around ventured to offer an opinion. "Hell, Bones, it might help if you had yourself a shower every once in a while!"

"Hey!" the biker protested, turning his attention away from Eden and onto the source of the insult. "*Tracker Jack* here ain't much cleaner than I am."

The lone barmaid, who had been trying to fight her way through the crowd with a loaded tray of drinks, finally got her two cents in. "Give it up, Bones. He might be a little messy at the moment, but with some men you just don't mind the dirt." She sidled her way up to Rafferty, smiling suggestively. "What'll it be, sweetie? The usual?"

Apparently taking the barmaid up on her advice, Bones rumbled off to drown his sorrows in another bottle of beer.

Jack turned to the waitress, who was plastered up against him as tight as peanut butter on jelly, and treated her to a slow, easy smile. "Sounds fine to me, Tina."

"Make that *two* usuals," Eden cut in boldly. "Please," she added, struggling to keep her temper. It wasn't the tantalizing Tina she was angry with at the moment. "I could use a drink."

"Suit yourself, hon," the waitress said with a shrug, reluctantly peeling herself away from Rafferty's side and turning to fill the order.

Jack gripped her by the arm and hauled her to a private table at the back of the room. "Have you lost your mind, *Ms. Wellbourne*? Sit," he told her, kicking out a chair and settling himself on a wooden stool directly opposite. "Just how naive are you, anyway? Don't you know that big bad boys like Bones eat uptown ladies like you for breakfast?"

Eden's chin went up defensively as she folded her arms across her chest and shot him a smoldering glare. "I'm still here, aren't I? And all in one piece, I might add, no thanks to you."

He studied her with some amusement. "That grateful for my help, are you? Face the facts, Ed. You'd be in serious trouble by now if I hadn't stepped in to protect you."

"Protect me? Ha! You were *pawing* me, and enjoying it just a little too much. You might've tried something more appropriate!"

"Fine." He laughed softly, leaning toward her across the small table. "Next time I want to make my mark on you in a rowdy, redneck bar, I'll kiss you instead."

"That's not what I meant!" she insisted, more affected by his sudden nearness than she was willing to admit. The scent of him enveloped her, assaulting her senses like a cloud of something dark and intimate, heavy with steaming male sexuality. Yes, sexual, that's what Rafferty's smell was. If she knew how to bottle it, she'd be rich beyond her wildest dreams. "I don't want you to kiss me."

He tucked a hand under her chin and let his gaze drift slowly to her lips. "Don't you, Ed?"

A sharp thrill raced through Eden at the thought that he might actually have the audacity to kiss her, right then and there! It was unsettling to realize that this man was capable of almost anything. Unsettling and somehow . . . fascinating.

"Of course not," she finally managed, slightly breathless. "Actually I was imagining you would punch Bones out or something."

Seeming to lose interest in her mouth for the moment, he shifted himself back on the stool again and propped his legs against the edge of the table. "Such violent fantasies, Princess. What do you suppose they mean?"

"I *wasn't* fantasizing!"

His expression softened faintly into a sexy, understanding, crinkly kind of a smile. "If you say so. But just for your information, Ed, I didn't go a few rounds with big Bones over there because it would've been a foolish thing to do. That boy has the body of a sumo wrestler and a brain the size of a peanut. I might've been able to take him on, but I might just as easily have had the bejeezus beat out of me. And then who would've been left to look after you?"

"I can fend for myself just fine, thank you."

"Could've fooled me."

"It's my fiancé I'm worried about," she continued, ignoring his comment. "Something urgent's come up.

New evidence that he's in terrible trouble. I came here to ask you to reconsider."

Judging by the look of resoluteness that flashed across Ed's face, Jack began to wonder if *he* wasn't the one in trouble. Despite all of his concerted efforts to send her on her way, she refused to give up. No doubt the lady was downright determined, not to mention nuts for following him into this dangerous dockside dump.

If he was going to be completely honest with himself, brutally honest, he had to admit to a certain amount of admiration for her persistence. There was a backbone beneath all that soft skin and sensuality, a double shot of starch inside the cute, feminine cut of her suit. But beyond that sense of appreciation he might have for her pure, unexpected pluck, Jack also felt a disquieting amount of fear.

He knew what could happen to women in this world who had no one to look after them. Anything.

Wasn't that what fate had held in store for Lara when he had failed to look after her? There was hardly a grim, grueling scenario left he hadn't played out in his mind in the search for his little sister. The possibilities were as endless as they were horrifying.

Hell, where was Ed Wellbourne's worthless fiancé, anyway? Why wasn't the stupid bastard here to take care of her?

Missing lovers. Of all the cases he'd handled, they were undoubtedly his least favorite. Invariably the situation would get messy. There was no limit to the seedy, sordid kind of details that could crop up in the course of the investigation, and the lady in front of him looked far too fragile to handle half of it.

"Look, Ed," he told her roughly, "be a good girl. Go home, do you hear me? Go to the police, the FBI, hell, call out the National Guard, just do yourself a favor and find someone else. Find *anyone* else."

"No," she said stubbornly. "There *isn't* anyone else, and even if there were, I don't have the time to waste to interview them. As for the police, they won't take me seriously, not even now."

"Now?" he demanded bluntly. "What's happened to make your search so urgent all of a sudden?"

Facing him squarely, she took a deep breath and calmly proceeded to recite the salient facts. "The perfume shop my sister and I own in Winter Park was broken into. It occurred less than an hour ago, about fifteen minutes after Hope closed up for the evening. It's been ransacked, Mr. Rafferty."

"Burglarized?"

"*Searched*," she insisted. "There was plenty of money left lying around, and it wasn't even touched. Not the petty cash box, not even the register. They didn't seem to want Hope's beautiful antique bottle collection either, even though some of the rarer examples are very valuable."

"Crooks with bad taste," he said. "There's nothing so unusual about that. As far as the money goes, maybe they were interrupted before they had a chance to make off with it."

She shook her head slowly, continuing to explain in a soft, rational voice why she didn't believe a simple burglary was the best explanation. "It takes thirty seconds for the alarm to sound in the shop and another minute before it's set off at the security company. If the security guys can't verify that it's a legal entry after five minutes or so, *then* they notify the police. Add several minutes minimum for the cops to arrive. That gives the burglars at least ten minutes to grab the cash and run.

Which in this case they didn't, despite the fact that they had plenty of time. Don't you think that's a little odd, even if the crooks were completely incompetent?"

In spite of his wholehearted desire not to become involved in the case, Jack reluctantly felt his interest begin to rise.

"They would've had to have bungled it pretty bad," he agreed. "But if you rule out money, what do you believe they were searching for?"

"Paperwork," she revealed. "Records, research. Or more specifically, *my* research. There was only one thing actually missing from the store as far as Hope could tell, and that was my personal workbook."

"What is it exactly you do for a living, Ed? Besides hounding PIs to death, that is."

She flashed him a brief smile. "I'm a "nose" for Armand's perfume company. Well, actually, it's his father's company, but Armand heads up the Product Development Department, where we put together ideas and formulas for new fragrances. He's the scientist, but my job is more intuitive, artistic. It's complex, a little like painting, or creating music. I guess you could say that I compose with scents and smells instead of notes."

"So your workbook was full of . . . ?"

"Formulas," she explained. "Floral combinations, essential oils I'd wanted to try out, nothing vital, just some ideas I was experimenting with."

He put a hand to his chin, scratching thoughtfully at the bristled beard he'd never consciously intended to grow. "Seems a bit coincidental that Herman and the workbook both disappear in the same week."

"Too coincidental," Eden concurred. "I can't help thinking that the two events are somehow connected.

They *must* be connected. Whoever broke into our shop knew exactly what they were looking for. And whatever it was, it's pretty clear they didn't find it. Yet."

Just when Eden was wondering if she'd made any headway with convincing Jack to come on board, Tina's sudden appearance at the table brought their private conversation to a temporary close.

"There you go," the barmaid said, neatly dropping a pair of topped-off shot glasses in front of them, miraculously managing not to slosh a single drop of liquid over their sides. "Couple of Purple Salvation Stingers. Good for the soul, if I say so myself."

Rafferty tossed a small wad of bills onto Tina's tray.

"Hope they work," the barmaid added with a wink.

Eden turned her attention to the small glass in front of her.

"Is something wrong with mine?" she asked. "It's not purple."

Tina laughed. "Don't you get it, girl? They make *you* turn purple, then pray for salvation."

"Oh," Eden responded, wondering if the "usual" order had been such a good idea after all.

An impatient roar from a rowdy bunch around the pool table summoned Tina quickly back to work. "Catch you later, Tracker Jack," she called over her shoulder before disappearing into the crowd again.

"Tracker Jack?" Eden repeated. "Is that what they call you?"

"Among other things," he admitted.

"Because you're good?" she asked impulsively, then flushed warmly as the unintentional meaning of her words sunk in.

"Lady," he said, grinning, "I'm *damn* good. At my

work. But it helps to be a local boy, born and raised. A native Floridian."

It was another factor in his favor, Eden realized.

"I can pay," she promised. "Whatever your going rate is, I'll come up with the fee, even if I have to sell my half of the shop to afford you."

The laugh he returned was harsh, self-deprecating. "I'm afraid just about anyone can afford me at the moment. I've got a few hefty medical bills hanging over my head. And a certain Dr. Gallamore who wouldn't hesitate to take my blood as collateral."

"Oh. You're not sick, are you?" Eden didn't think she'd ever seen a healthier looking man in her life.

"I'm fine," he said matter-of-factly, staring contemplatively down at the table in front of him.

Indeed, his physique appeared to be incredibly . . . sound. Even beneath all the grit and grime. Since he wasn't watching her just at that moment, she took the opportunity to check him out thoroughly for the first time.

She let her gaze start at the top of his windblown hair and slowly work its way down. As far as she could see, Jack Rafferty's body looked to be remarkable. Muscles seemed to be rippling everywhere, even though he wasn't doing anything more strenuous than kicking back on his barstool. Long, bulging cords of them crisscrossed his torso, wrapped around his shoulders, snaked along his upper legs and thighs. It was the parts she couldn't see that continued to draw her attention, especially those that were right in front of her but still hidden from view.

With his legs propped up on the table, his dirt-caked jeans, threadbare in strategic spots, were practically staring her in the face. Small tufts of blond body hair curled from several of the rips and tears, and certain muscles were so boldly mesmerizing, so totally male, that she couldn't seem to tear her eyes away from the riveting sight.

"The bills were for a . . . family member," he explained, looking up.

Eden flushed, caught in the act of staring—at body parts she would never even have the nerve to think about, not to mention *gape* at.

"Why?" he asked coolly, his eyes narrowing in amusement at her very unprofessional interest. "Concerned about my job qualifications?"

"No," she protested adamantly, still embarrassed beyond belief at her own inexplicable behavior. "No, I was just wondering about your current state of physical health and your stamina."

"My *stamina*? Trust me, Princess," he said, flashing a smooth smile, "I'm exactly like that little toy rabbit when I get wound up. I just keep on going and going, as long as I'm needed."

"Oh! Well," she said inanely, striving to regain some semblance of control, "I'm sure you're more than . . . adequate."

His sexy smile widened to a grin. "So I've been told."

She needed a drink, Eden decided. Without further hesitation she reached for her shot glass and downed the searing stuff in a single swallow. Her eyes widened in surprise as the alcohol burned a sizzling path to the pit of her stomach. The coughing started shortly afterward.

"What—what *was* that? Lighter fluid?"

"Close." Jack laughed and reached over to slap her helpfully across the back. "You okay, Ed? Sure you don't need a chaser?" he suggested considerately. "Or a doctor?"

Still struggling for breath, she lifted her head again, eyeing him squarely. "I need you to take my case."

He ran his hands through his hair, staring at the ceiling, then settled a stern, warning gaze back on her. "Look, if you'll lay off for a while, I'll make you a deal. I'll drop by the shop with you and have a look around. See if I can come up with anything."

"Sounds perfect to me," she told him, feeling better already. "When do we leave?"

Before Eden had a chance to fully comprehend what was happening, she found herself back at Rafferty's houseboat again. Only this time she was standing inside his living quarters instead of outside his front door.

"This isn't exactly what I had in mind when I agreed to lay off for a while," she said, looking curiously around the surprisingly spacious room as Jack disappeared through an open doorway. "I'm not sure I like the idea of just hanging around here while you take a shower."

"You're welcome to join me," he said amicably from the next room. "I don't mind sharing."

"Thanks anyway," she shot back boldly, "but I think I'll pass."

In fact, if she ever needed to bathe that badly, she'd rather take her chances in the gator-infested lake outside than share a shower stall with the likes of Tracker Jack. Swimming with a bunch of hungry reptiles sounded a whole lot safer than getting wet and naked with a man like that.

At the sound of the water beginning to run, she

breathed a quick sigh of relief and turned her attention back to her surroundings. A sliding glass door, with what she had to admit was a fabulous lake view out back, seemed to be about the only attractive thing the place had going for it. The rest of the decor seemed to be pretty much male minimalist.

A comfortable couch that looked like it had seen better years, a desk in the corner, piled high with file folders, an up-to-date computer system, and a cell phone.

A holstered handgun draped across the back of a leather swivel chair.

So Rafferty was armed, was he? Probably licensed to carry a concealed weapon. Eden wasn't sure if that made her feel better about her decision to hire him, or worse. One thing was certain, he seemed to be a man of few distractions. There was no television, no CD player, not even a single sports or pinup magazine to be seen anywhere in the room. In fact, there were very few items around that didn't have something to do with his job. Clearly the guy was incredibly serious about his work. Pared down, focused—maybe even a little obsessed.

She felt Babette stirring restlessly inside her handbag and bent to put the little dog on the floor for a few minutes of exercise. The poodle stretched, shook herself out, then set about exploring the new patch of territory. Padding daintily around the room from one end to the other, she made a point of pausing to smell everything, barked at the couch for a bit, then discovered a laundry basket in the corner with a pile of Jack's clothes beside it.

Eden apparently wasn't the only one who had picked

up on Rafferty's scent. But instead of barking at the male stranger's smell, Babette proceeded to settle herself comfortably at the center of the small clothing heap.

Feeling a little woozy from the effects of the drink she'd had, Eden was almost tempted to settle down on the couch herself, but the sound of Jack's voice behind her stopped her short.

"Stinger started to hit you yet, Ed?"

Eden whirled around to face him, making herself dizzy in the process, but the moment she managed to bring him into focus, she had the shock of her life. She wasn't sure if it was the booze, or the stress, or the unexpected sight of a clean, towel-clad Jack Rafferty, but *something* hit her just then. Hit her hard.

"Oh!" was all she could manage to say, but *Oh dear* was what she was really thinking inside. *Oh Lord*, she added silently.

Oh no!

It was miraculous, really, what a little soap and water could do. The man in front of her barely resembled the grimy, grungy, grit-covered PI she'd met earlier. There was no more sand, no more dirt, no more dark, bearded stubble obscuring his face. There was nothing concealing his body, either, except for a small stretch of terrycloth, slung low and snug, strategically knotted at the corner of his hip.

Fresh out of the shower, Jack Rafferty was scrubbed and buffed all the way down to his burnished, bronzed skin, with steam still rising from his sinewy shoulders.

Eden swallowed hard, broadsided by the sight of him. The slick, dripping, sexy sight of him.

No, she promised herself, she *wasn't* going to pass

out, no matter how weak her knees were beginning to feel, no matter how dark the room was starting to grow.

"Hold on there, Ed," he cautioned, and stepped forward to catch her before her body hit the floor.

THREE

Eden opened her eyes and found herself flat on her back, staring up into Tracker Jack's face. For heaven's sake, now that his beard had been shaven away, the man was a sight that would make any nice southern girl swoon.

Not that she believed that was what had happened to her. There were other, more obvious reasons she had fainted all of a sudden. The alcohol, for instance, coupled with the fact that she hadn't eaten a bite since that morning. The stress of the situation, combined with her oversensitive constitution. Of course, the man leaning over her with a look of concern in his riveting green eyes had nothing to do with it.

Still, she'd be lying to herself if she didn't admit that Jack was good-looking. In a bold, devastating sort of way. If it was possible to look beyond all that shamelessly exposed brawn, she might actually find him to be handsome.

Eden fervently reminded herself that she far preferred clean-cut, competent, black-haired scientists to barbarous, roughneck blonds. Blonds who didn't know how to behave themselves. Such as the one who was almost on top of her, starting to do things with his hands she definitely didn't approve of. Like inserting exploratory fingers into the neckline of her blouse and touching them expertly to the cleft of her throat.

"What do you think you're doing?"

"Hold still, Princess. Just checking for a pulse."

A pulse? Eden knew for a fact that hers had just skyrocketed. "I still have one," she assured him, squirming quickly out of reach.

"What's the matter, Princess?" he asked, his voice smooth and low, with a throaty hint of roughness underneath. "My bed isn't soft enough for you?"

"Your bed?" Eden glanced around, horrified to discover exactly where she'd regained consciousness. Not on that well-worn living room couch as she'd first imagined. Instead she was nestled as snug as a bug in Jack Rafferty's bedroom. Smack dab in the middle of his bed.

Worse, he was still bending over her with all the fascinated intensity of a dog on a bone, watching her every move. For mercy's sake, he was barely even dressed. And she did mean *barely*.

"I told you I don't mind sharing," Jack said.

Eden quickly lifted her eyes again. "Sharing?"

"Southern hospitality, remember?"

"Hospitality?" she squeaked, scrambling quickly off the bed and safely out of Rafferty's reach. "That isn't the sort of help I had in mind when I came here to hire you."

"Ed," he said, laughing softly, apparently amused by her hasty retreat, "relax. I'm not in the habit of taking helpless women to bed and pouncing on them. At least not after they've passed out. I'd rather take them to bed first, have them faint afterward."

"Then what am I doing here?"

He cocked a wry smile at her. "You'd rather be sacked out on my living room floor along with that donut-sized dog of yours?"

"Babette!" Eden exclaimed. "Is she okay?"

"Okay?" Jack repeated. "She's about as high-strung as you are. Luckily, though, she's still sleeping at the moment. Seems to have taken a strange liking to my clothes for some reason."

Eden let out a quick sigh of relief. "Speaking of clothes," she said, "maybe you should go put some on. You promised to stop by the shop, remember, and Hope might not appreciate it if you showed up looking like— well, like *that*." She waved her hand in front of her, indicating the general direction of his mostly naked, brazenly beautiful male form.

Then again, she thought wryly, maybe Hope *would* appreciate it.

What sane woman wouldn't?

The minute she set foot in the shop again, Eden took one look at her exhausted older sister and begged her to go home. "Please, Hope," she said, stepping forward to greet her with a much-needed hug as Jack entered the showroom closely behind her. "It's obvious you've had enough to take care of for one night. Mr. Rafferty and I can handle it from here."

Hope cast an inquisitive glance Jack's way, taking in every detail of the PI's roguish, decidedly fascinating form and face. Eden couldn't blame her for her curiosity.

His size alone seemed overwhelming within the confines of the narrow front room, making everything else seem smaller and more fragile by contrast. A single swipe from one powerful arm could send a hundred fine bottles scattering across the polished wooden floor. One swift kick of his strong leg would easily topple the tall, gilded étagère of glass.

"You come highly recommended, Mr. Rafferty," Hope said without preamble. "Do you think you can help my little sister?"

"I can try," Jack came back, parrying her directness with a slow Southern drawl. "But I don't make promises I can't keep."

"A man of your word, are you?" Hope asked with an approving smile. "That's a rarity nowadays. If there were more like you in the male population at large, I don't think we'd be in this predicament."

"Hope!" Eden exclaimed. "Do you hear what you're saying? It sounds like you're blaming Armand."

Jack cast a questioning glance at her sister. "Is that true?" he queried her sternly. "Do you think this guy got himself lost on purpose?"

"I don't know what to think anymore," Hope said. "I've never met the man, myself. But the invitations have been sent, the initials embossed on the napkins, everything perfectly planned and in place, right down to the dinner mints, and still there's no sign of a groom. Something very weird is going on, and in my experience that means a man must be responsible for it."

"Whatever it is," Eden said, "it isn't Armand's fault."

"If you say so," Hope responded doubtfully. "But for now, I'm going to take you up on your advice, Eden, and leave you two to figure it out." She made her way to the front door, yawning. "I've had about all the intrigue I can handle for one evening. Good night, sis."

"Talk to you in the morning," Eden said, and locked the front door behind her. She plopped Babette safely on top of her favorite feather pillow, then turned to face Rafferty again, wondering what to say about her sister's apparent lack of faith in her fiancé.

"Wedding invitations already went out, huh?" he inquired softly. "Monogrammed dinner napkins? Mints? Guess your sister's thought of everything, hasn't she?"

She folded her arms in front of her, going quickly on the defensive. "Don't make fun. Hope's been working really hard to get everything ready."

"Why's she so concerned? It's your wedding, isn't it?"

Her chin went up, her whole body bristling at the PI's unparalleled audacity. He had no right to attack Hope. "Of course it's my wedding," she said angrily. "But Hope's been almost like a mother to me since our parents divorced. I was really too young to remember it all, but my mom was a basket case for a long time after Dad ditched us. Hope practically ended up raising me herself. Watching me get married, well, maybe it will make it all worth it for her. This ceremony means a lot to her."

He lounged back against the showcase, studying her. "Don't get your pantyhose in such a bind, Princess. I was just wondering. Are you sure this ceremony's going to mean half as much to you?"

"Don't you see?" she said, frustrated by his apparent lack of comprehension. "Hope lost her faith when my father bailed out, but I didn't. I still believe in happily-ever-after. At least when it's with the right man. My marriage to Armand will make everything okay again."

"Is that why you're getting married, Ed? To prove that all men are not pond scum?"

"Of course not! Look, how did we get on this subject, anyway? Don't you think we ought to be searching for clues instead of discussing my personal relationships?"

"If you say so. Where do you want to start?"

To be honest, she wanted to start by planting a fist across the smug, stubborn set of Jack Rafferty's jaw. Where did he get off questioning her about her feelings for her fiancé? He was supposed to find Armand, not dig into all of her intimate thoughts about marriage and commitment.

"You're the investigator," she shot back. "You tell me."

"Show me around. If I want a closer look at anything, I'll let you know."

She continued with the tour through the shop.

"Here's the bottle collection I was telling you about earlier," she said. "Nothing's been removed, even though some of the examples are fine enough to be considered museum quality."

She was happy for Hope's sake that it was all still there, each sparkling piece in its untouched, pristine state, perfectly aligned on shelf after shelf of illuminated, dust-free glass. The assemblage of shapes and colors was so gorgeous, so rare and stunning, that customers came from miles around just to get a glimpse. In fact, no jeweler's case could hold a candle to it.

The scintillating spectrum of hues ranged from the palest cameo pink and cut-glass rose to full-blown reds and violets. There were blues in shades from morning to midnight, greens as cool and soothing as a summer forest, rich oranges and yellows that glimmered softly into gold. The forms, too, were as fabulous as the colors, each sensual container a tactile, touchable sculpture unto itself.

Eden had seen the collection a thousand times, but its sheer visual impact still had the power to take her breath away. "Lovely, aren't they?"

"Yeah," he said, his voice low and unexpectedly quiet. "Beautiful."

Eden glanced his way, surprised to see his gaze focused directly on her instead of the bottles. Flustered, she forced her attention back to the tour, leading him toward the back room.

She stepped inside the compelling, sweetly familiar space, taking a deep breath as Jack followed closely behind. She had grown up the well-worn old room, with its high, spacious ceiling and stone-covered floor. It had been her childhood hideaway, tucked away from the world, forgotten by time.

Forgotten by everyone but herself. Her mother, as well as a long line of previous shop owners, had used it for storage. Eden had used it to escape.

Her playthings were still there, all the old objects she'd discovered, the odd remnants that had collected from the turn of the century to the present day. The apothecary jars with their worn, gold-etched labels, and remains from the pharmacy that had once stood in this same spot were still there. The glass globes filled with fancy-colored waters, and the musty boxes of dry and crumbling dusting powder, their perfume faint from decades of decay were still there too. Her happiest, most vivid memories were of rummaging through all the junk and jars for the few treasures that remained, the bottles and vials still half full of strange, unfamiliar smells.

Their vivid pungency had the power to transport her to places that she'd dreamed of as a child.

"I used to hang out here as a kid," she explained, reluctant to tell Jack exactly what the room had meant to her back then. She wasn't even sure if she could describe it. "I've used it as my office and temporary laboratory for the past few weeks, ever since I returned from Paris. That's my desk over there, the table with the papers strewn all over the place. It wasn't like that when I left earlier."

Jack let out a low whistle as he looked around, trying to get a general feel for the place. *Interesting* was the word that about summed it up, followed closely by the term *mysterious.* So this was where Ed had spent her childhood, was it? Seeing her in this element for the first time, he was beginning to get a hint of what Ms. Wellbourne was all about.

He'd figured the bottle collection in the front was a pretty good indicator of the older sister's personality. Perfectionistic. A caretaker. Of things, and people too. But if Hope had handled their childhood traumas by trying to arrange their lives into clean, careful order, was this how Ed had managed to cope? By shutting herself off from the rest of the world and turning her attention inward?

No wonder Ms. Wellbourne's senses had become so exquisitely sharpened.

She had honed them herself, become attuned to the little things that other folks might not notice. Like the smell of a soap bar made to pamper the pale skin of some delicate Victorian lady, or the sensual touch of a satin sachet. All designed for a world far different than today's, for women whose responsiveness hadn't been anesthetized by the frantic speed and frenzy of modern society. For a woman like Ed, temperamental and touchy, but demonstrative and intensely deep-feeling.

A woman so emotive that a man had only to look at her to incite an impassioned, white-hot response.

Don't go there, man, Jack warned himself silently, feeling his own responses being drawn down a dangerous path.

He forced his attention back to the table she'd indicated, wishing like hell he'd never agreed to follow her. "So where was the notebook?" he asked.

"Top left drawer," she said. "It wasn't locked, but I really didn't see any reason to."

It didn't take an experienced eye, Jack realized, to see that the desk had been thoroughly searched. Every drawer had been rummaged through, its contents carefully scoured, then upended or scattered at random. But what had the bad guys been looking for?

Behind all the papers, propped up along the back of the desk, was a wooden form of some kind that Jack didn't recognize. U-shaped and full of shelves that ascended in height, it made him think of a miniature football stadium, with hundreds of small amber bottles assembled like fans in a scaffold of bleachers.

He picked up one sealed, spice-jar-sized vial and attempted to read the hand-lettered label. *Propionate de Benzyle.* He reached for a second, curious to make out the meaning of a name he'd never heard before. *Chypre.* "*Patchouli,*" he managed, reading the neatly scrawled word from the front of a third vial. "What is all this?"

"My instrument," Ed explained, "although it isn't musical. It's called a perfume organ. Those jars are the keys to the scents I compose."

"*Lavandre, Santal.* Ed, there are hundreds of them.

Is this how you keep track of all the ingredients you're working with at any one time?"

She stepped up to the organ, lightly running her hands across the glass jars with their strange-sounding contents, as if the act of touching could call up each raw fragrance in turn. "Not exactly. The memories are all here," she went on, placing a fingertip to her forehead. "Thousands of smells, like recollections of sensations running around in my head. I don't start by blending the fragrances together or sampling them, or even running tests. I begin by remembering."

Jack whistled softly, impressed. The lady's brain was even more intricate than he'd first imagined. In fact, if she had the ability to create from pure imagination, to paint from a palette made only of memories, she was obviously downright talented. "Thousands of scents, huh? And you manage to remember them all?"

"It's part of my job to commit aromas to memory. A summer evening when the grass is freshly cut. A smoggy winter morning in the city. A crowded subway. A Christmas tree. I've been trained to pick and choose the best ones, to create new combinations."

Jack put the bottles down again and began to pace slowly back and forth across the hard stone floor.

"These formulas you create," he said, thinking out loud, "they must be worth a fortune to the company you work for."

"Millions," she agreed. "Tens of millions if the work is good. Maybe more if it's great. The scent that Armand and I just finished is expected to be just that when it's launched. Great."

He stopped, raked back a stray handful of hair from his forehead. "So how does the company handle security issues? Corporate espionage, that kind of thing. I mean, if they've got a piece of paper with a cash-in potential of twenty million dollars or more, that's a pretty tempting secret for a competitor to steal."

"True," she said, "but the House of Guillon guards its treasures jealously. Security is so tight that no single person at the company is ever entrusted with a complete formula in written form. The teams that work on a fragrance are given only pieces of the equation a little at a time. And only on a need-to-know basis."

"What's to stop someone from remembering it all?" he asked. "Someone like you, for instance."

"Too complex," she said, shaking her head. "The combinations are elaborate, extremely detailed. I doubt one person could do it. In the case of our new formula, for instance, I'm holding on to half of the equation, and I don't think I could even recite that much from memory if I had to."

He walked closer to her desk, stopping directly in front of it. Somewhere there were the pieces of the puzzle he needed. All he had to do was make sense of them. "But your half of the formula was *not* in the missing notebook?"

She sighed gratefully. "Thankfully not. It's still locked securely away in a safe deposit box at the local bank, exactly where I left it. But no one else knows that, not even Armand. It's also highly possible that the existence of the new scent was leaked to the rest of the perfume industry. Unfortunately, spies are rampant in my business. I wouldn't put it past one of our competitors, like Scentsations, to have sent someone here from France to try and steal the recipe."

"Sounds plausible to me," Jack agreed, "especially if millions are at stake. But according to what you're telling me, the burglars wouldn't have succeeded in hijacking the formula even if they had found your expensive little slip of paper."

"Exactly. The scent can't be re-created until *both* parts of the original document are combined."

He turned back to face her, drawn by the connection that was finally beginning to form in his own head. "So if you're holding one half of the record," he said, his gaze dropping to hers, connecting her thoughts with his own, "who's hanging on to the other?"

"Armand," she said softly, her voice lowering to a worried whisper. "Now do you see why I'm so concerned?"

Sure, he saw it all right. What he intended to do about it was another matter entirely. "I don't blame you for worrying, Ed. Herman could be in serious trouble."

But he wasn't the only one, Jack added silently. Ed herself was at risk, too, although she didn't seem to realize it. Yet.

Her voice dropped to a barely audible murmur. "Do you think he's been kidnapped?"

"Can't say for sure, Princess. At this point anything's possible."

If someone had made off with the fiancé to get to the formula, Jack reasoned silently, they'd already discovered he held only half of it. Presumably they'd broken into her shop looking for the rest of it. Which meant there was one place left to search—Ed's person.

She could be in serious danger.

Jack swore softly, struggling with his conscience and his common sense, searching for the strength he needed to turn around and walk away. From Ed Wellbourne and all of the problems she'd presented him with. Not the least of which was temptation, strong and simple.

Yeah, she tempted him, with her wide amber eyes,

her schoolgirl bravado, and her very grown-up body. But it wasn't her upscale brand of beauty that interested him the most.

It was the part that was unreachable, carefully protected from sensation, guarded like one of her costly perfumes sealed within a gorgeous, glittering bottle. Glass walls. They were all around her, erected from years of practice. Jack wondered what it would be like to shatter those walls and release the lady's sensual side.

Hell, he didn't have to wonder. He *knew*.

The same instinctive way he knew that Herman was not the right man for her.

No, a brainy, clinical chemist was the last man he'd pair Eden up with. She'd as much as admitted to a telltale lack of passion, at least on her part. If she really believed that friendship and camaraderie were a decent substitute for love, she was sorely deluded. Still, she needed to find the guy, if only to figure that out for herself.

And Jack knew he was going to help her do it. He *had* to help her. The memory of how he'd left Lara alone still weighed heavily on his mind. He'd deserted her by going off to school. He was personally responsible for that particular tragedy, and he wasn't about to stand by and let another one happen.

"Don't look so sad," he said, taking her firmly by the shoulders and giving her an easy, encouraging shake. "If you're willing to finance the case, I'm willing to take it for my usual fee, but I'll need a five-hundred-dollar retainer up front. Like I told you before, I'm flat broke."

"Fine," she responded. "No problem."

"And there's another condition."

"Anything." She looked up at him with so much

gratitude, it made Jack's heart go suddenly soft around the edges.

Now, why did she have to go and gaze at him like that? he wondered. As if he were her savior somehow, instead of the backwoods, hard-living, barely surviving excuse for a human being he knew himself to be. Body hunting was the only thing he'd ever been good at, and one glance from Ed Wellbourne was enough to lay even that on the line. He wasn't sure he could live up to his reputation this time, not without breaking the single most important rule of any PI case.

Never become personally involved.

It was the cardinal sin of a tracker's career, and for the first time in his life Jack was inclined to commit it. This assignment wasn't going to be easy with a client like Ed under his wing. Or under his roof.

"You'll have to come with me," he told her bluntly. "Hide out on my houseboat until your fiancé returns."

Anything, Eden thought silently, but *that*. "You're kidding, right?"

He tucked a hand under her chin and tilted her head up until she had a good look at his face. "I'm not smiling, am I?"

"You mean *live* with you?" she asked. "Cohabit?"

He dropped his hands back to his sides, releasing her with a soft, easy laugh. "If that's what you want to call it. But it's the only way I know how to protect you from the people who did this to your shop. From the same thing that happened to Herman."

So he *did* believe that Armand could have been kidnapped for the formula, Eden realized. In which case the plan made sense, considering the bad guys might decide to come after her next. Still, for some strange reason the thought of being held for ransom wasn't half as scary as the idea of shacking up with Jack Rafferty.

"No, thanks," she said firmly. "I'll just have to take my chances living at Hope's until we find him."

"Fine. But in that case you'll have to find him alone. No protection, no deal."

Eden felt herself being gradually backed into a corner. "It's apparent," she said, clearing her throat, "that we've reached an impasse."

He cocked a blond eyebrow at her.

"So," she continued, ignoring the expression, "I'd like to suggest an alternate proposal. Another offer. I suggest that we keep in close touch instead of actually living together."

"Close touch, huh?" He backed her slowly toward the wall, pinning both of her arms helplessly over her head as he brought his face within inches of hers. "How close did you mean, Ed? Like this?" he demanded, bringing his entire body against hers, pressing her hard up against the plaster. "Or maybe like *this*." His lips hovered so near, she could almost taste them.

Sardines, Eden decided, weren't packed any tighter than she was at that moment to Jack. She was, so to speak, between a wall and a hard place. Or more accurately, a hard body.

There wasn't a single part of him she couldn't feel against her, from his chest and abs to his hips and thighs. He was giving her a graphic, hands-on lesson about how a man was made. In fact there was only one part of him that *wasn't* touching her. His mouth.

Strangely, that separation made Eden want to feel him there even more. The tension became unbearable, breathless, until the only thing left on her mind was the thought of what he was going to do to her with that mouth.

In a last-ditch effort to save herself, she closed her eyes and forced herself to speak. "Actually," she whispered, "I was thinking more along the lines of cell phones. Calling each other a few times a day. That sort of thing."

She felt a warm rush of air against her face and then nothing. He'd let her go. She opened her eyes, just in time to see him heading for the exit.

"Enough, Ed," he called back to her. "If that didn't just prove to you how vulnerable you are, nothing will."

Oh Lord, she was vulnerable all right, but not only to the bad guys who might be after her. She was vulnerable to him, to the way her body responded when he did those terrible, terrible things. He hadn't even kissed her, and still her knees had been ready to melt right out from under her. One look into those hot, hypnotic green eyes and she'd nearly forgotten her fiancé's name.

Armand, she reminded herself silently. It's Armand!

"I'm history," he added, his hand on the door.

It was an awful ultimatum he was giving her, Eden realized.

It was the sheer, overwhelming guilt she felt that finally decided her. Guilt for even *wondering* what it would be like for Jack Rafferty to kiss her while her faithful fiancé could be in danger at this very moment. If Armand could survive a kidnapping by a bunch of bad guys, she could certainly survive a few days or so on a boat with a bad boy like Jack.

Couldn't she?

FOUR

"Stop!" Eden called out after Jack's rapidly retreating form. "You win. I'll go with you."

He stopped in his tracks, turning around to face her. "As long as we understand each other."

"What about Hope?" she asked him.

"She'll have to close the store for a week or two," Jack told her. "I'd suggest sending her off on a long vacation. She seemed pretty overworked, anyway. It's probably the best thing for her."

"Agreed," Eden said, sick of arguing.

"Very sensible of you, Ed. See how much simpler things are when we don't fight?"

"Simple for *you*," she said. Certainly nothing about the situation seemed simple to her.

As for agreeing to sail off into the sunset with Jack— that was closer to sheer insanity than good sense. A small boat. A big man. A desperate woman. The possibilities were too ominous to contemplate.

"You can pack tonight," he instructed her. "Make arrangements with Hope, then meet me at the lake in the morning. "We leave at sunrise."

———◆————————◆———

A cool morning mist was still hovering over the lake when she arrived. With the sun just coming up over the sparkling, moist treetops, Eden sensed the day breaking beautifully around her.

Jack's reaction to the early hour wasn't quite as enchanted. In response to Eden's knock, he swung the door open, squinted at the bright shaft of sunlight that was glittering through the trees, and stretched himself out, yawning. Looking sleepy, rumpled, and sexier than any man should be allowed to, he nodded a gruff hello, confiscated her suitcase, and motioned her inside.

"Coffee?" he growled, unceremoniously depositing her bag at the end of the couch and heading for the pot that was percolating on the small kitchen stove.

"Thanks," she murmured, reaching for the cup. "And a fine good morning to you too."

He raked a tousled wave of hair from his eyes and took a long, appreciative swallow from his own oversized cup. "Give me a break. I'm still waking up."

"Uh-huh. And on the wrong side of bed, apparently."

The grin he gave her was boyish, cocky. "Right, left. Either side of the sack suits me just fine." He downed another dose of his morning brew, his audacity growing as the sleepiness wore off. "What about you, Ed? Which side of the hay do you like to . . . snooze on?"

"Which side do I— Look, Rafferty, I don't see how that's the least bit relevant to our search."

He shrugged. "Just thought you'd want to cover the sleeping arrangements right off. It's a one-bedroom boat, remember?"

Did she remember? It was a fact she had very little

hope of forgetting. The recollection of the cozy room was already etched indelibly in her memory.

"You're not suggesting. . . ? Get real, Tracker Jack. I'd just as soon rough it on the floor as bunk down in that bed with you."

"You sure about that, Princess? Because the boat's not heated and spring nights can get pretty cool on the river."

"Look, I appreciate your concern for my comfort. But you could steer this barge all the way to Alaska and I still wouldn't be sleeping next to you. The couch will be just fine for me."

"Suit yourself."

"In fact, it's probably best that we lay a few more ground rules right from the start. After all, this isn't a pleasure cruise. The quarters might be close, but there's no reason we can't keep our personal privacy intact. I suggest we shower at alternate times, as well. I'll wash in the mornings, you can have the evenings."

"Maybe you'd like to draw a line down the center of the boat, too, just to make sure I keep to my half."

"Now that you mention it . . ."

"Look, Princess, I told you earlier I'm not in the habit of taking women against their will. And even if I was, you'd have nothing to worry about. You're not my type."

"Oh," Eden said, unsure whether to be insulted or relieved. "Well, good, then," she said, setting her purse down on the floor as a sign she intended to stay. "At least we're agreed on that point."

Before he had a chance to answer, Babette poked her head out of the bag, wrinkling her nose as she sampled the air around her.

"What," Jack demanded, "is *that* doing here?"

"*That*," she responded protectively, "is my dog, remember? You didn't expect me to leave her behind, did you? She's terrified of being left alone. In fact, it's one of the few things she's truly afraid of."

"Kennel her, then. Being boarded with other animals will give her plenty of company. Although I doubt they'll recognize her as a fellow canine. Looks more like a dust bunny than a dog. About as useful too."

"I can't kennel her," she explained firmly. "She spent her whole puppyhood in a small, sterile cage. When I adopted her, I swore I would never let anyone lock her up like that again."

He seemed to hesitate then, blinking down at the little dog with an expression that looked suspiciously similar to compassion. Was it possible, Eden wondered, that such a tough man had a heart made of anything but solid rock?

"She was a lab animal," Eden said softly. "If you've ever had a dog of your own, I know you'll understand how I feel about that. Have you ever had a dog?"

Jack stayed silent for what seemed like a very long time, then finally responded, "Yes. Up until yesterday."

Eden blinked hard at the unexpected answer. "Oh. Your dog died? I'm so sorry."

"Don't be," he said gruffly. "Wolf had a long life. And the end, when it came, was easy for him."

"For *him*," Eden said, "but what about you?"

"Me?" he asked, as if the idea of considering his own emotional state was a completely foreign concept. "I'm left without the best tracking partner a PI ever had. Wolf was a mutt, but he was fifty pounds of the smartest, sharpest mutt you've ever met. A working dog," he added, looking doubtfully down at Babette as if to reinforce the contrast.

She wasn't fooled for an instant. It was obvious from Jack's tone that the animal had been much more to him than a working tool. He'd loved his dog, that much was clear. Beneath Rafferty's cool, I-can-take-it exterior, there was a core of emotion that clearly ran deep.

"Babette might not be trained to work," she said, "but I promise she won't be a bother. You might even grow to like her."

"It's doubtful." He eyed the small furball grudgingly. "Just keep her out from underfoot," he added, reluctantly giving in.

"Of course," Eden agreed, slightly miffed by his stern tone and cold, albeit practical words. He was, after all, still in mourning for his own dog, although he wouldn't admit it. And any man who'd loved an animal that much couldn't be all bad, could he?

Jack worked his way to the open bow of the boat, wondering exactly how he'd caved in so easily to Ed Wellbourne's wishes. It really didn't make a helluva lot of difference to him whether she brought her frilly, froufrou animal along or not, but the fact that she'd gotten to him so quickly, that did bother him. Stowing the anchor, he released the boat from her mooring and prepared to cast off.

"Can I help?" her voice sounded behind him.

"No, thanks," he said, positioning himself behind the steering wheel and cranking the engine up to idling speed. "I can handle it from here."

"No doubt," she murmured dryly. "But you might at least fill me in on where we're headed."

"A tracker's job usually starts where the trail grows cold," he explained. "In Herman's case, that means the orange groves where he was last seen. The area's accessible by water, about a day's journey northwest from here, straight across Lake Jesup and up into the St. Johns River. With any luck we'll arrive late this afternoon and still have an hour or two to look around before sunset."

"Sounds logical," she said, "but I can't imagine what sort of clues we might find just by visiting an orange grove. How do you know what to look for?"

"Experience," he said matter-of-factly, "along with fifteen years of on-the-job training. I've picked up a few tricks since graduating from PI school."

"A school for private investigators?" she asked. "I didn't realize there was such a thing."

Neither had he, Jack admitted silently, until he'd needed to find every scrap of information he could get his hands on. Until the police had left him hanging and desperate, hungry for any sort of hope of finding his sister. He'd begged them for help, pleaded for more to be done, but there hadn't been enough money to expend more than a minimal amount on the case.

Nor had his family, poor and worthless, had enough pull in the community or political clout to compel the cops into further action. Frustrated by the ineptitude of the authorities, Jack had vowed to do their job himself. Unfortunately, Lara's trail had grown cold long before he'd learned enough to be of any use to her.

And now the cops called on him for help when a case got too tough for them to crack. Ironically, the police hired Tracker Jack because they knew he was the best in the business at turning up bodies. Every body, that is, but one.

"Yeah, there's a school all right," he said. "But

there's only so much they can teach you. The rest has to be learned the hard way."

He opened the throttle up, urging the motor to an easy crawl, and expertly guided the craft clear of the dock and out into the open lake. He felt the wind whipping lightly against his face as he eased the engine up to cruising speed. Then the shore fell away and the familiar pull of freedom took hold of him.

Along the far strand of beach a heron launched itself into the air on sleek blue wings, compelled to escape the confines of gravity. The unseen force that seemed to beckon the bird forward was the same one that urged Jack onward.

The need to keep moving, if only to survive.

"How beautiful," Eden said as she followed the line of his gaze and caught sight of the soaring bird.

"A great blue heron. We probably startled it."

He glanced up at the sky again. "Looks like it's going to be a scorcher by early afternoon."

"Oh, I came prepared for that. Plenty of sunscreen. Lots of bottled water. I even dressed in layers." She pointed down at the open collar of her pale cotton blouse where a bright shock of brilliance could barely be seen. The shimmering purple fabric of her bathing suit top.

Jack found himself staring at the orchid-colored outline with a fascination that was as undeniable as it was involuntary. After a lifetime spent in the woods and fields and wetlands, he thought he'd faced every danger the central Florida wilds had to offer.

He'd been wrong.

Reaching into the front pocket of his safari-style shirt, he retrieved a pair of sunglasses. Ms. Wellbourne might have prepared herself to face the sun in sensual style, but a good tracker was equipped for any emergency. And as far as Jack was concerned, that small purple bathing suit top definitely qualified as an emergency.

His all-weather, all-terrain shades were unusually dark, designed for the roughest of conditions. Unfortunately, they weren't quite dark enough.

The top of her blouse was still buttoned, concealing most of the undergarment from his view, but that only made the sight of it more provocative. It was a vision that left a man wondering, made him speculate about exactly what was hiding beneath.

Much to Jack's perturbation, it wasn't too long before he found out. True to his prediction, the temperature climbed steadily throughout the morning, rising to the mid-eighties sometime around noon. By two o'clock his own shirt was damp with perspiration that had nothing to do with the heat of the sun and everything to do with Ed innocently stretched out on the bow of his boat. Sporting not only the top of her two-piece but the bottom as well.

It was a sight that left him struggling for air.

Arousal pulled deep in the pit of his stomach. Damn, but she was beautiful. One look and she'd left him aching. But it wasn't simply Ed's easy-on-the-eyes appearance that interested him to the point of pain.

He'd seen bikinis before. What was it about this particular woman that made him want to do much, much more than just look?

Whatever it was, one thing was certain. She was way too fine for a man like him. Sexy as sin, too, although she didn't seem to know it.

Why didn't she know it? Jack wondered. Why hadn't the brilliant Herman made that fact very clear to her? Damned if he understood, but he did know this—if she was *his* woman, there would be no doubt in her mind about it.

She turned to look at him just then, meeting his gaze with a suddenness he wasn't prepared for, catching him off guard. Catching him in the act of ogling.

Not that Jack minded. In fact, her reaction to his stare was every bit as arousing as the rest of her. Her eyes fluttered for an instant, the pupils dilating in response to his glance. The irises flared to a golden simmer, taking on the sweet, hot color of flame-warmed whiskey. One-hundred-proof passionate, that's what Ed's eyes were. More seductive than a double shot of Southern Comfort.

Tension stretched between them, wire taut, until Ed finally broke the gaze and glanced away.

"Look out!" she shouted.

Jack looked up to see the shoreline rushing suddenly toward them. Swearing softly under his breath, he quickly steered the boat to a safer distance.

"Sorry for the rough ride," he said, recovering control. Ruthlessly he reminded himself where his attention ought to be at the moment—navigating the narrowing stretch of river instead of Ed's bikini. On the case at hand, not on her.

Eden nodded back at him, her heart in her throat. Was it the close call with the river's edge or the sudden awareness between them that had set the butterflies loose in her stomach? She'd known good and well that Jack's eyes were on her. He hadn't simply been watching her, he'd practically been devouring her with that all-consuming green gaze of his.

And she had allowed it.

No, it was far worse than that. She'd actually encouraged it. Heaven help her, but she'd enjoyed every moment of his languorous, lingering stare.

Heavens, what had come over her? Never in her life had she so blatantly displayed herself to a man. But then, never had a man looked at her in quite that way, as if she was the last drink of water in the middle of a desert.

Not even Armand.

A wave of guilt washed over her, compelling her to slip her shirt and shorts back on with lightning speed. She had no intention of risking another encounter with raffish Jack Rafferty's gaze. Trusting her case to him was one thing. Trusting her body to him was another matter entirely. Especially in a lush, secluded, incredibly private setting like this where she didn't even seem to be able to trust herself.

Maybe *that* was what was wrong with her. The exotic serenity of the jungle-rich riverbank had caused her to get carried away. Clearly it was the surroundings that had come over her, not the man she was experiencing them with.

Before she had a chance to consider the problem further, a new sensation floated over her, a cloud of fragrance so heady and overwhelming, it washed every other experience temporarily from her mind. The perfume of full-grown orange blossoms.

"Oh!" she exclaimed, closing her eyes and drinking it in, "we must be getting close to the groves."

"Still a few miles away," Jack said. "You can detect them at this distance?"

Detect them? The aroma was already so rich and enchanting, it was making her weak at the knees. "The fragrance. It's . . . incredible."

It was exactly a mile and a half upriver before Jack

caught his first hint of the fragrance. The scent was incredible all right, but while most folks might be drawn to the sweetness, it was a smell he had learned to hate. He frowned briefly, trying to relegate the aroma, along with his unpleasant reaction to it, to the back of his mind.

"You don't like it," Eden said, reading his thoughts or his body language, he wasn't sure which.

"No," he agreed curtly, "I don't. It's too sweet for my taste. Too cloying. Too . . . familiar."

She·nodded, seeming to understand his repugnance. "Associative recollection. There's nothing like a vivid smell to call a distant scrap of memory up in your mind. There have been studies done that show the olfactory sense is an ancient one, deeply and directly connected to certain human emotions."

Emotions? A man in his position couldn't afford the luxury of emotions. He'd been trained to track his quarry with a method as dispassionate as was humanly possible. Personal feelings could only get in the way of his work, cloud his reactions, possibly even prove lethal to the person he happened to be searching for.

Then, too, there was the matter of simple self-preservation. If he'd stopped to grieve for every client whose case had been hopeless, he'd have burned out on investigating long ago. An unhappy ending, he reminded himself, was better than no ending at all, and Jack had seen more than his share of them.

"It reminds you of something, doesn't it?" she prodded. "The smell of the orange blossoms. What does it make you think of?"

"Lay off, Ed," he warned her, not wanting to go there.

"Sorry!" She held her hands up in a gesture of mock surrender. "Jeez, you ask a simple question and . . ."

"Look," he went on, sorry for scaring her, but at the same time not being able to stop himself. "You wanted to know what emotion the memory is connected with? Well, you got it. It's anger, Ms. Wellbourne, plain and simple. The very smell of the place makes me sick."

It was his father, Jack realized suddenly. His old man was the person that scent made him think of. The place had been another orange grove, the time so long ago, he thought he'd forgotten. Hell, he couldn't have been much older than six or seven, but still, there was a reason he remembered. . . .

Ah, yes, the pain. His arms had been bleeding from the scrape of the thorns, his whole body stiff and sore. And yet, it was the cut to the heart that had hurt him the most.

"I'm sorry for intruding," Ed whispered, "but you really ought to talk about it. Anger isn't something you should keep all bottled up inside."

He cast her a long, curious glance. "What would you know about that?"

"Not much personally," she explained, "but I've seen what it did to my mom as well as to Hope. They've never let go of their anger at my father for leaving. Maybe I wouldn't have been able to either if I'd been older at the time, but at least I've been able to move on with my life. Letting go has helped me move forward. It might help you too."

"Talking about bad things doesn't make them go away, Princess. It's not that simple."

"It might just make them a little easier, though. Besides, how do you know if you've never tried?"

Ed Wellbourne wasn't just talented, Jack decided,

she was eerily intuitive. She had detected the emotion inside him almost as easily as she'd caught the smell of the orange blossoms. Feelings he'd spent years trying to distance himself from, he could not hide from her.

"Who is it you're angry at?"

"My old man," he told her finally, hoping that she'd drop the discussion, leave it at that. She didn't.

"What did he do?"

She was asking for it, Jack decided. All the sad, seamy facts. It was best that she heard them, anyway, best that she knew what sort of man he was up front, what kind of background he'd come from. That way, the next time he came anywhere near, she might have the good sense to slap him away.

"It was late in winter," he said, struggling to recall the smallest details. "The fruit was ripe. Sticky and sweet with smell. And my father, on one of the rare occasions when he actually worked, took me with him to the groves to pick oranges for pay."

The thick, sugar-laden juice had run down his face and arms, mingling with the blood, but the discomfort had barely bothered him. At that age, Jack's hero had still been his dad. He would have done almost anything to please him.

He'd been so proud of himself for beating out men three times his age. His father, on the other hand, had stayed sullen and silent, picking no more fruit than a single basket himself. Never offering Jack a single word of praise.

"The old man probably needed some extra cash," he continued, "and whoever owned the groves didn't bother with little details like child labor laws. I must've picked two dozen bushels that day, but fifty dozen wouldn't have been enough to satisfy my dad. No wonder the memory's still intact after all this time. It's the first day I realized what my father really was."

"I don't blame you," she said softly, "for hating the smell."

God, yes, he hated it. Just the memory of the rotting, overripe fruit and its stinking, floating clouds of perfume had the power to make him sick to his stomach. He still despised the old man, for deserting his wife and daughter as much as for anything else.

"It's history," he said, shrugging it off as he steered the boat toward a man-made seawall and prepared to dock.

Past history, he added silently to himself, but a useful reminder of the sort of man he was today. The lowbred son of a sniveling, no-account bum. The wrong sort of man for a lady like Ms. Wellbourne.

The wisest course of action would be to remember that the next time she sported that purple spandex mantrap in front of him.

But then, Jack rarely did the wisest thing. . . .

FIVE

"Yeah, I've seen the guy all right," the farmer said, squinting hard at the snapshot that Jack flashed in front of him. "Foreign fellow, right? Wearing a three-piece suit in the middle of my orange grove. From Russia, was he?"

"France," Eden corrected him gently.

"Oh, France, eh?" The older man glanced suspiciously at the four-by-six, glossy rendition of Armand's serious face. "Knew he was some kind of foreigner. Spent a good hour here doing nothing but asking a lot of questions about the crops and taking down notes. Bit of a pencil-head, isn't he?"

Jack shot the farmer a cordial grin. "You *have* seen him, then."

"A pencil-head?" Eden repeated, indignant. "He is no such—"

Jack silenced her with a warning stare, then turned his attention back to the grovekeeper. "That's the guy," he confirmed. "Tall geek. Talks funny."

"*Geek?*" Eden seethed hotly, jabbing Jack in his overdeveloped abs. "Of all the—"

"Acts odd too," the older man affirmed. "More interested in the flowers than anything else."

"Weird as a lake loon," Jack agreed heartily.

Before Eden had the chance to protest again, Babette popped her head up out of her bag.

Snapping on her leash, Eden let her down to explore the immediate area, but Babette seemed to have other ideas. She walked as far as the short lead would let her, then strained against the confines of her collar, crying pitifully.

"Something wrong with your pup, lady?" the farmer asked, not unkindly.

"I don't know," Eden answered honestly. "She seems to want to go to that tree stump over there." Wisely giving in to the squirming poodle's wishes, Eden let herself be led to the short, sawn-off trunk.

Babette circled the stump slowly, stopping in certain spots to paw energetically at the ground, then barking excitedly at the scent she had stirred up.

"Funny," the farmer said, "but that's exactly where pencil-head sat while he was writing all those notes."

Babette picked that particular moment to add a new act to her repertoire. After scratching and barking in each fascinating spot around the stump, she squatted to relieve herself, marking her chosen area with a dainty, well-directed stream of dog urine.

"Oh dear," Eden said. "Do you suppose—"

"Suppose what?" Jack asked.

"Well, I know this may sound funny. It's an unfortunate tendency, very embarrassing, but that's exactly what she does whenever she gets around Armand's shoes."

"You mean she—"

"Pees on them," Eden confirmed. "Whether Armand is in them or not."

Jack shot an amused grin down at the industriously urinating poodle, wondering if there wasn't something to like in the clockwork-toy animal after all. She'd picked up on the fiancé's scent pretty quick, a skill that could prove useful in their search. Further, she clearly didn't care much for the erudite Armand.

Whether Babette's telling reaction to Herman was learned or automatic, it was a sentiment Jack was beginning to share. A dog's instincts were usually right.

"What do you two want with this fellow, anyway?" the farmer asked. "Is he in some kind of trouble?"

"He's just turned up missing," Jack said.

"Tourists," the farmer said distastefully. "Should've known the guy would get into a situation when I gave him directions to that Jungle joint. Bad sort of place, but he insisted."

"The Jungle?" Jack repeated, looking mildly surprised. "You sure that's where he went?"

"Far as I know," the farmer said. "Least, that's the last I've seen of him."

Jack thanked the older man for the information, then stood silent and thoughtful as the farmer turned to leave.

"That's it?" Eden demanded. "Don't you have any more questions for him?"

Jack shrugged carelessly. "Nope. He's already told me everything I needed to know."

"But— Look, Rafferty, I don't get it. He tells you Armand has disappeared into some jungle and that's the end of it?"

"Not some jungle," Jack said, correcting her. *"The*

Jungle. It's a well-known nightclub and hotel not too far from here."

"Oh. A hotel. Well, good, then. Armand must've been planning to check in there for the night."

"Maybe. At least it's a solid lead."

"Maybe? Why would he ask for directions if he didn't intend to stay there?"

"Sorry to have to tell you this, Princess, but most men that go to The Jungle aren't simply interested in finding a place to spend the night. In fact, after an evening in the nightclub, sleeping is usually the last thing on their minds."

Ed's eyes widened slowly in disbelief. "Just what sort of establishment is this Jungle place, anyway?"

"A unique one," Jack informed her, "with a reputation for fantasy-style accommodations and on-the-edge entertainment."

"On the edge of what?"

He lifted his brow, eyeing her uncertainly. "Let's just say that the floor show is said to be . . . erotic."

Ed folded her arms across her chest and shot him an incredulous stare.

"Armand," she said firmly, "would never set foot in a place like that."

"If you say so."

"Not in a million years," she insisted. "Not the Armand I know. He's far too sensible. Too—"

"Straitlaced?"

Ed's chin went up defensively in stubborn response to the unflattering description. "All I'm saying is, if he did go there, he would've had to have had a very good reason."

For the life of him Jack couldn't imagine what that good reason could be. Several bad ones, however, came easily to mind. For starters the fiancé could be stepping out on her, as he'd first surmised. Or it could be worse.

The Jungle was a known pleasure palace for all kinds of silk-tie-sporting creeps to take their women to—women who were usually not their wives. It was also the sort of hangout in which borderline businessmen and other suit-clad criminals liked to meet to make shady deals. In which case Herman might have been lured there by the same underworld element that broke into Ed's shop.

Either way, they had no choice but to follow up on the lead.

"If that's the case," he said, "there's only one way to find out exactly what Herman's good reason was. First thing tomorrow we'll check the place out for ourselves. By checking *in* to the hotel."

Exactly how, Eden wondered grumpily, did she get herself into these things?

She found herself seated in the enormous, open-air lobby of the most exotic, albeit classy hotel she'd ever seen, facing the prospect of shacking up with a man she'd met only two days before.

Yes, shacking up. It was the only polite way to describe what Jack Rafferty's brilliant plan involved. *Sharing* a room together. Eden's heart rate went a little wild just from the thought of it. The alarming, strangely frightening thought of it.

She hadn't even agreed to the harebrained plan, and yet here she was, waiting quietly and obediently with Babette while Jack made discreet inquiries at the front desk. She rolled her eyes to the ceiling, where a thatched, palapa-style roof soared fifty feet or so into an arched architectural fantasy. A circle of pygmy palm trees surrounded the perimeter of the room, providing some measure of protection from the outside breeze as well as a gorgeous green backdrop for the parrots that preened in the bare branches overhead. There was nothing subtle about the place, but it was much nicer than Eden had first imagined.

Babette certainly seemed to like it, exploring every inch of the floor space that the length of her leash would allow. The bright, fluttering parrots were a source of particular fascination that she could barely keep her gaze off. Until Jack strolled back into sight.

Eden watched in amazement as her little dog greeted him with all the tail-wagging excitement and enthusiasm of a long-lost buddy. To her further amazement Jack actually greeted Babette back, bending to brush a quick, friendly swipe across the top of her tiny, tufted head.

"Any luck?" Eden asked eagerly, standing to meet him. "Did they have any record of Armand staying here?"

"Sorry, Princess, but nobody's talking. Yet. Got us a room, though. Or rather, a bungalow."

Eden swallowed hard, not liking the sound of that. "A bungalow? You mean we're going to stay here anyway, even though no one's seen him?"

"Come on, Ed," he chided her, in his low, sexy Southern drawl, "you're not going to give up that easily, are you?

"I am not giving up! I just don't see why two bungalows aren't better than one. Tell you what," she said, brightening. "I'll go reserve us another." She turned to make her way toward the front desk.

Jack stopped her short with a single, swift tug on the back of her short cotton shirt. "Whoa, there. Just where do you think you're going? I thought we settled all this earlier."

"*You* settled it," she said, spinning back around. "But I still don't like it."

Not one bit, she added silently. A room was bad enough, but a bungalow? The very word called up visions of a lurid hideaway, complete with satin sheets, a heart-shaped bed, and who knew what other sort of sensual, suggestively-styled furniture. A love shack, she thought, shuddering.

"It's too late to make changes," he informed her. "It would blow the cover I came up with."

She frowned, almost afraid to ask. "What cover?"

"The best one to suit our purposes," Jack explained calmly. "I hinted around that we were lovers."

"Lovers?" Eden whispered, horrified. "You and me? I mean *us*?"

He took a short step forward, quickly closing the distance between them as he looked down at her intently, thoroughly searching her face. "Us, Princess. Why does the thought of that scare you so much?"

"Scared?" she squeaked faintly. "Do I look like I'm afraid?"

His interested gaze glanced over her again, taking the scenic excursion this time. "Yeah," he said finally. "You do."

Body language. Rafferty seemed to be able to read hers like a book.

"My feelings aren't the issue here," she said, vainly attempting to change the subject.

"Good, because you're going to have to get over

them if you want to get Herman back. Either that," he said, "or face them."

What was he asking of her? To admit that his very nearness was enough to make her knees want to give out from under her, that her heart pounded wildly every time he got close, that the simple scent of him made her tremble with instant awareness? *Never*, she thought frantically. She wasn't even willing to admit it to herself.

"I can see how it wouldn't be wise to reveal our true identities," she said, "especially since we're going to be pumping the locals for information."

Jack nodded. "Folks tend to get suspicious when they know a PI is nosing around. Makes them clam up unnecessarily."

"But really, you might at least have come up with something more believable. It's obvious that we *don't* go together. I mean, we're such opposites."

"Opposites attract, Ed. Just don't look at me that way and I'm sure it'll work out fine," he said.

"What way?"

"Like you'd hit the top of this ceiling if I touched you."

"I would not!"

"Wanna bet?"

"Go ahead," she dared him defiantly.

Jack's eyes narrowed dangerously. "Don't tempt me, Princess."

"Do it," she said recklessly. "Touch me. Kiss me. Make mad, passionate love to me. I can handle it."

The silence stretched between them, and Eden held her breath. Had she really challenged him to do those things? Had she completely lost her mind?

"Shall we see about that?" Jack asked warningly.

Pressing her up against one of the wide wooden columns that supported the soaring roof, he anchored both of her arms helplessly by her sides and proceeded to prove that she would lose control with him.

His kiss, when it came, was potent and punishing, effectively penetrating every last barrier she'd tried to erect against him. She was lost instantly, conquered by the searing strength of it. She gave a sudden, silent gasp as her legs began to buckle beneath her. The need to breathe became secondary as he thoroughly mastered her, blotting every emotion, every feeling from her mind except one.

Desire. Devastating, all-consuming desire.

"Princess," he murmured, his hand stroking urgently against her face, "open your mouth for me."

Eden willingly obeyed, shocked by the soaring sensation she felt as his tongue swept deep inside her. Excitement stirred within her, sweet and sharp, as her stomach clutched crazily in response to his touch. To the raw, primitive power of a force she had no strength to resist.

An anguished sigh escaped her as Jack deepened the kiss, merciless in his urgent ministrations. The sensations grew stronger, spiraling wildly out of control as he continued to explore her mouth with his tongue, rhythmically probing the warm, dark recesses until she wanted to weep from the dizzying pleasure of it.

A pleasure that wasn't entirely her own. Jack, too, seemed to be caught up in the kiss as his own arousal became physically evident. He was rigid against her, terrifyingly hard, and so huge, it scared Eden senseless.

Oh dear, was that what she had done to him? But even more alarming was the realization of what he wanted to do to her. Everything.

She didn't doubt he was capable of following through with it. How was she going to stop him?

Mercy, she wasn't sure she wanted to!

Jack checked himself with an effort, drawing back from Ed's mouth, more shaken than he cared to admit. One simple kiss, that's all it had been, and he was aroused enough to take her that second. To make crazy, urgent love to her as they stood, and to let the consequences of his actions be damned.

Her eyes were wide and dreamy looking, almost drugged with desire as they fluttered open, blinking in hazy confusion. Deep muscles pulled tight at the base of his body as he struggled to regain some control. Blood pulsed brutally through his veins and arteries, pounding with an energy so powerful, it was closer to pain than pleasure.

Yeah, he wanted this woman all right. Wanted her bad, if the testosterone surge in his body was anything to go by. And judging by the way she gazed at him, she wanted him too.

Her lips were parted, her skin softly flushed, giving her a wild, abandoned appearance that was erotically at odds with her uptight personality. Half temptress, half uptown lady with a don't-touch-me look. And both parts of her sexy as sin.

Jack had to admit to a certain level of satisfaction at proving his point so thoroughly. She had lost control with him.

But then again, so had he.

He reminded himself roughly of the complications any involvement with this lady could cause. She was engaged, for starters, but that wasn't the stumbling block that worried him the most. Being a fiancée was a far cry from being someone's wife. In fact, to Jack's way of thinking, any woman was fair game until she actually tied the knot.

No, it was his own personal involvement rule that warned him to stay a safe distance. Problem was, the only way to put enough real estate between him and Ed to make things really safe would mean making tracks for the next state. He couldn't do that to her, not since they'd already come this far in the case.

Still, one passionate kiss between two consenting adults didn't necessarily constitute personal involvement. One mind-blowing kiss, he thought, fascinated by the memory. Or maybe two . . .

He was just about to tip her head back and taste her again when a soft, shaky moan escaped her. Mistaking the sound for a cry of unhappiness, Babette began to bark at him in protest.

The sudden, insistent noise brought Ed to her senses again and made Jack swear roughly under his breath.

"Traitor," he said, glaring down at the dog in amused frustration. How was he supposed to get anywhere with a woman who had her own watch-poodle monitoring his every move?

"Poor baby," Ed said a little breathlessly to Babette, then glanced shyly back up at him. "Guess she thought you were trying to hurt me."

He shook his head slowly. "I would never do that, Princess."

She folded her arms across her chest, recovering her composure along with her stubbornness. "Then maybe you'd better not kiss me again."

Jack narrowed his eyes at her, stung by the words.

What the hell did he care if she wanted him to kiss her again or not? Hadn't he just been trying to warn himself about all the potential perils she posed for him?

"Admit it, Ed," he said roughly. "You liked it as much as I did."

"I'll admit that I *invited* it."

"Baby, you were begging for it."

"I had my reasons," she said defensively. "The cover, remember?" She glanced quickly around the largely deserted lobby, almost as an afterthought. "I'll bet there's not a person in this place who doesn't believe we're lovers now."

He laughed harshly. "So it was all an act, then? Is that what you're trying to tell me? Because you sure didn't like the idea of going along with the cover before."

"I changed my mind," she insisted.

"I see. There's only one problem with that, Princess. No one saw us kissing."

"What are you saying?"

"That I might have to do it again, Ed. Whether you like it or not. For the sake of the case, that is."

"Oh. Well, but only if it's absolutely necessary. And only in public. That's the rule."

"Only in public, huh?"

"Yes, no touching in private. No kissing. No nothing. Especially not while we're in the bungalow."

"Fine," Jack said quietly. "Just remember, you made the rules."

"What do you mean by that?"

"Nothing. But if I can manage to keep my grubby paws off you in private, I'll expect for you to put up a good act in public, okay?"

"Well—"

"It's no more than you've already done, so it shouldn't be a problem, should it?"

"I guess not."

"Especially since we both know we're *not* going to be lovers. Don't we?"

SIX

When they entered the bungalow, Eden hesitated at the threshold, where, to her amazement, the lurid decor she'd been expecting did not materialize.

Instead of the crushed-red-velvet theme she'd so vividly imagined, the entire spacious hut was done up in a subtle and sophisticated jungle motif. It was oddly disconcerting to discover that there wasn't the tiniest bit of tackiness to be seen.

"Not bad," Jack observed, tossing their bags into the spacious walk-in closet and settling himself comfortably in a plump, Pappasan chair. He propped his long legs on the coral-colored stone coffee table. "Man could get used to this kind of life."

"Well, don't get too used to it," Eden said, inspecting the room. "Hopefully we won't be staying long."

She had to admit, the place really wasn't bad. In fact, it was downright beautiful. Cream-colored satin-covered walls. Pale, hand-painted furniture. Tile floors softened by a matched set of cut silk rugs.

But the bed was undoubtedly the focal point. Sleek

and luxuriously simple, its enormous size certainly drew the eye.

Worse, it was the only possible place to stretch out on in the room. With the exception of two chairs, both of which were far too small to sleep in, there was no other furniture in the room.

One bed, two adults. Those were dangerous odds as far as Eden was concerned.

"Bed's really something, isn't it?" Jack asked, breaking into her thoughts almost as if he'd read them.

Oh, it was something all right, she agreed silently. Something awful. Settling Babette in the center of the remaining chair, she dropped her purse down beside it and strode purposely for the phone. "Hello, front desk?"

Jack was beside her in seconds, wrapping his hand firmly around the mouthpiece as he stopped her conversation with a single, warning whisper. "What do you think you're doing?"

"Calling for a cot," she explained in frustration, trying to pry his fingers from the handle of the phone. It was about as easy as untying a knot of steel cables.

"Are you nuts?"

"Not at all," she insisted, still tugging at his hand. "I happen to like the idea of sleeping on a foldaway mattress."

"Right," he said, obviously amused. "No doubt it would do wonders for your back. But it would also give the hotel staff the wrong idea. Sorry, Ed, it's out of the question."

He took the phone from her, easily deflecting her efforts to snatch it away. "Yes, front desk? We'll need reservations for the nightclub this evening. Table for two. Seven o'clock."

She folded her arms across her chest, frowning suspiciously as he cradled the receiver again. "I thought the plan was to gather further information, not step out on the town for the night."

"The plan's still in place, Princess. Can you think of a better spot to dig up dirt than the local lounge?"

"Well, no. But I doubt Armand would go there."

"Ed, it's the main attraction. Everyone goes there."

His words were starting to make sense, which seriously worried her. "If you say so."

He arched an eyebrow at her in surprise. "Agreeing with me so easily? Sure you're feeling okay?"

"I guess it's a good plan. Just don't forget it's business, not pleasure."

"You have some pretty weird rules, Princess. Hope you won't have to break any more of them."

"What do you mean any more? I haven't broken any."

"Sure you have. Not two minutes ago. You touched me."

"Oh. On the phone. I guess I did, didn't I?" She'd barely even been aware of doing it, which meant either that she was getting used to the idea of physical contact with this man, or worse, that on some unconscious level she was actually seeking it out.

"Kinda hard to keep your hands off me, isn't it?"

"Very funny. I can promise you, it won't happen again."

"Don't make promises you can't keep, Princess," he warned her, heading for the door.

"Where are you going?"

"To get some air. Don't worry, I'll be back in time to pick you up for our big date."

She was just about to remind him that the evening

would not remotely resemble a date, but before the words would come, she was talking to air. Babette jumped down off the chair and trotted to the door, barking unhappily over Jack's sudden disappearance.

"Don't tell me you miss him already," Eden said, grumbling at the unapologetic poodle, "because I don't even want to hear about it."

Babette barked again, then settled herself directly across the entrance threshold, stretching her fluffy paws in front of her.

"Going to wait for him right there, are you?" Eden asked the little dog. "Haven't you ever heard of playing hard to get?"

The poodle's head dropped to her paws, but her ears remained on the alert, listening hopefully for any sound of the returning Rafferty.

"Apparently not. But I'd better warn you not to get too attached to him. He's not the sort of man to stick around for long."

Babette closed her eyes, apparently unconcerned about the pending potential for doggie heartbreak she was unwisely exposing herself to.

Eden sighed heavily. "I know, you don't want to hear it, but there's no sense in falling for a loner like that. No safety. No security. He'll probably just pack up and leave as soon as the case is solved."

Babette yawned, either bored with the entire lecture or annoyed with Eden for keeping her awake. Her body language seemed to say, *Are you still talking? Why don't you give it a rest, Mom, and let me sleep?*

"You're *not* falling for him, are you? Because it would be scandalous of you to forget about Armand so quickly. I know he's never been one of your favorite people, but aren't dogs supposed to be loyal no matter what?"

One of the poodle's eyes opened momentarily. Eden wasn't entirely sure, but she thought that if Babette could speak, she would've asked, *Aren't fiancées supposed to be loyal too?*

It was a question for which there was no easy answer.

Leaving Babette to rest by the door, Eden headed for the bathroom with her cosmetic case in hand, deciding she'd better take advantage of the relative privacy while she still had the chance. The Jacuzzi was enormous and elegant, beckoning her to soak her worries away.

She turned the faucet up full force, found a bottle of foaming gel in a nearby basket, and emptied the contents under the steaming stream of water. By the time the cloud of bubbles reached the marble rim of the tub, she had carefully closed the bathroom door, quickly undressed, and slipped blissfully into the silky, perfumed water. For the first time in days she felt warm and wonderfully relaxed.

For the first time since she'd met Jack Rafferty, that is.

The mirrored wall behind the tub caught her image, reflected it back to her in the sensual, softly lit surroundings.

Touching her fingertips to her lips, she caressed herself absently, reliving the shocking moment when Jack had kissed her. She'd never really expected him to do it.

She'd never expected herself to respond so wantonly.

The sensations returned as she stared in the mirror, vividly recalling the effect he'd had on her. The effect he was still having on her. A sudden spillway of excitement stirred deep in her belly, as shimmering and swirling as the soft currents of water that were lapping around her. Jerking her hand away, she drew her knees to her chest, hoping to hug the feeling away, but nothing could stop it completely.

Nothing, that is, except following through with it and finding out where the unfamiliar feelings would lead. She couldn't deny that there was some small part of her that wanted to do just that. To fall headlong into further physical intimacy with Jack and brazenly explore her responses.

Of course, she *couldn't* do any such thing. Armand was the only man she'd ever been to bed with, mainly because she'd never taken such things lightly. She'd been friends with him long before they'd become lovers.

But she also couldn't help being the least little bit curious. If one kiss from Jack already had her so off balance she could barely breathe, did it logically follow that making love with him would be equally explosive?

Physically it would be totally terrifying. Her very sensitivity would make her feel the experience more powerfully than most. The pain of it as well as the pleasure. And even if she did manage to get over the physical hurdles, the emotional issues were equally treacherous.

As much as she wanted to experience a physical climax, she did not want to have it without emotional commitment. And Jack Rafferty was the least emotionally available man she'd ever met. So far he hadn't even let her get close enough to find out why.

He'd only let her close enough to kiss her.

A situation she promised herself would not happen again.

Ducking under the water to wash her hair, she scrubbed, rinsed, and surfaced to the sound of his voice.

"Ed?"

Oh dear. Was he back already?

"Ed? Where'd you disappear to?"

"In here, Rafferty," she called out quickly. "I'm in the tub. Don't you *dare* open the door!"

"Another dare, Princess? What makes you think I won't take you up on it this time?"

To Eden's horror the door began to open, inch by inch, the squeaking hinges protesting in place of the scream that refused to rise from her throat. He really was going to walk in on her! But just as she thought the door was about to burst open, it stopped short. And instead of Jack Rafferty standing before her, only his arm appeared. An arm with a large rectangular box dangling from the end of it.

"What—what is that?" she asked, cautiously submersing herself in bubbles up to her neck.

"A present," he said, tossing the mysterious box onto the marble-topped bathroom counter.

"Oh!" To her immense relief, the arm withdrew, disappearing again as the door closed quietly behind it. "Thank you," she called out, beginning to breathe a bit easier. "I think."

Curious, she stared at the unexpected package. What on earth? For the life of her she couldn't possibly imagine what was in it.

Spurred on by a sudden, childlike sense of excitement, she slipped from the tub and toweled off, wrapping herself in a luxurious terrycloth robe, compliments of the hotel. Twisting a smaller plush towel around the top of her head, turban-style, she reached for the box. It was beautifully wrapped with a wide satin bow. Almost too lovely to open, but after a moment's hesitation she carefully untied the ribbon, pulled back the lid, and looked inside.

And saw a dress the color of dark chocolate, smooth and long and so deliciously silky, it almost made her mouth water. Holding the fabric to her face, she stared in the mirror, noticing that the midnight shade set off her hair so perfectly, it looked as though it had been made to match.

Had Jack known that when he'd chosen it? she wondered. The gown was more dramatic and luxurious than she might've chosen for herself, but gorgeous nevertheless. Wistfully she folded it back into the box.

"Jack," she said, cracking the door, "I'm sorry, but there's no way I can keep this."

"What's the problem, Princess?"

She hesitated. "It's just too . . . personal."

"Personal? Maybe, but practical too. In fact, it's a necessity if we're going to check out the nightclub. There's a serious dress code in place. No grunge allowed, jackets required, that kind of thing."

Eden's eyebrows went up. A dress code? Well, maybe that did change things a little, especially since she'd neglected to pack anything nice enough for an evening out.

A sudden thought struck her. "Do you even own a jacket?"

His low chuckle sounded from the opposite side of the door. "I do now."

This time Eden's curiosity really did get the best of her. Apparently she wasn't the only one he'd gone shopping for. Jack Rafferty in a jacket? So far she hadn't seen him in anything more formal than denim. From the way that denim fit his narrow hips and firm backside, she'd reached an undeniable conclusion. Tracker Jack was born to wear blue jeans.

Anything else seemed completely out of character for him. At least, that's what she imagined before she popped her head around the door and caught a glimpse of him all dressed up. Dressed to kill. For the first time in Eden's life she understood what the expression meant. Jack in jeans was bad enough, but in a dark blue sport coat and crisp white shirt tucked into those jeans, the effect was downright devastating.

The cut of the coat was so streamlined and form-fitting, it looked as if it had been custom-made. Either that, or painted on with broad, masculine brush strokes. The smooth swath of fabric that stretched between his shoulders seemed to go on for miles, accentuating the power and strength of the physique that lay beneath. Blond, storm-swept hair contrasted boldly with the blue-black color, spilling nearly to his collar in a wind-blown waterfall of gold.

Eden's breath caught as she looked at him. God, but he was beautiful, dangerously so. One glance into those private eyes of his and a woman might forget who she was searching for. One glance and she might just as easily forget herself.

"Do I look presentable, Princess?"

Presentable? He looked handsome enough to break hearts. The nightclub was going to be littered with them.

"Fine," she lied, congratulating herself for how calm and in control her voice sounded. "I'm sure you'll pass the dress code with flying colors."

A quick, cocky grin flashed as he studied her speculatively. "I'm not so sure I can say the same thing about you."

"Thanks a lot!" she said, then put a hand to her head as she remembered the towel-style turban. "Oh. Guess I'd better get dressed."

Shutting the door again, she proceeded to apply her evening makeup. Piling her dark hair high on her head, she secured it into a smooth, sophisticated twist, then added a pair of dangling earrings that just grazed the nape of her neck when she moved. Her garter belt came next, along with a pair of pure silk stockings, one of the small luxuries she'd brought back with her from France. The dress was last, the final stage in her preparations, and she slipped it over her head, letting the silky fabric slide its way down her body until the hemline reached nearly to the floor. Turning to survey the results in the mirror, she looked herself over.

And had the shock of her life.

She'd thought the dress would be sleek and simple, maybe even a little subdued in its styling. She'd been wrong. What had appeared to be a perfectly innocuous piece of cloth in its beautiful presentation box had taken on a whole new look as it slithered its way down her figure. A clinging, sexy look.

For heaven's sake, the thing had more curves than a Monte Carlo racetrack, not to mention its own built-in air-conditioning. It seemed there were slits nearly everywhere, revealing sensual stretches of naked skin up the sides, down the front, even straight down the center of the nearly bare back. Either the seamstresses at the factory had forgotten to close a few seams or the designer was a frustrated sushi chef with a fetish for slicing and dicing.

I can't wear this was her instantaneous reaction to the outfit. It was too racy, too revealing, too much dress for a modest woman such as she. Or rather, it wasn't *enough* dress.

"Are you decent yet?" Jack called out to her.

No, she thought in stunned, silent shock. *I'm definitely not decent.*

His knock at the door was insistent. "You okay it there, Ed?"

She certainly was not okay. She was positively thunderstruck at the idea of being seen in such a garment. Unfortunately, she didn't have too long to think about it. Just as she was considering the possibility of crawling under the counter and hiding there safely until hell froze over, Jack opened the door and walked in on her.

"What are you—" He stopped dead in his tracks, seemed to struggle for air, then let out an appreciative whistle.

A wolf whistle. The kind no man had ever had the inclination to give her before.

"Whoa," he said. "Lady, you look dangerous."

However she appeared, Eden doubted that the word *lady* applied any longer.

Now, she thought frantically, was the perfect time to protest, to insist that she was not setting one stocking-clad foot outside in a garment so skimpy it made her bikini seem modest by comparison. But for some strange reason, she didn't do any such thing. Brushing past Jack into the bungalow, she rummaged through her suitcase instead, located a pair of strappy silver sandals, and slipped them on.

Babette bounced and barked in sudden protest, wisely recognizing that the shoes were a sure sign of her mistress's imminent departure.

Eden stooped to reassure her. "Be a good girl while we're gone," she said, and was rewarded for her efforts with a warm, wet tongue to the face. A lick that smelled suspiciously of—hamburger?

She frowned at her pet. "What have you been eating?"

She hadn't expected an answer from the poodle, but the response that came from Jack was almost as surprising. "Chopped sirloin," he admitted reluctantly.

"Chopped— Where did she get her paws on that?"

"Carry-out," he explained, shrugging. "From the restaurant."

Eden's eyebrows went up.

"Well, I couldn't let the scrawny thing starve, could I?" he asked her, going instantly on the defensive.

"Certainly not," she agreed, hiding a smile.

"One missed meal and she's liable to waste away."

"Uh-huh," Eden said diplomatically.

Babette settled herself on a comfortable pillow and curled up like a bagel, still licking her petite poodle lips.

"All set?" Jack asked, offering Eden his arm.

"Ready," she said, and held out her hand.

If the bungalow decor had slightly disappointed Eden for its sheer lack of decadence, the Jungle nightclub did not. Done up in the dark, daring theme of a rainforest at night, it was anything but understated.

The primitive sound of jungle drums throbbed steadily in the background. Mist swirled in streaming wisps around the room, ebbing and flowing with the damp evening air and the movement of the crowd that had already gathered.

A hostess appeared through the mist and ushered them to a palapa-topped table for two. A waitress followed shortly, wearing a skirt the size of a postage stamp and toting a fresh tray of tropical drinks. Jack's head inclined briefly as he engaged her in conversation, but the constant background beat as well as the intermittent birdcalls and strange screeches that sounded throughout the room prevented Eden from overhearing. It was a full five minutes before the woman walked away, leaving a pair of cocktails on the table in front of them.

Jack handed her a glass, and as she took it from his hand their fingers touched, barely brushing. Her gasp was muffled by the nightclub noise, but the startled movement she made was all too noticeable.

"Sorry," she said, setting the drink back on the table and rubbing her hand as if she'd been stung.

"No apology necessary," he told her. "We're in public, remember? Touching's allowed. In fact, as I recall, it's mandatory."

Grabbing again for the tall, cool cocktail, Eden took a long, fortifying sip, praying silently that the alcohol would calm the skyrocketing rate of her pulse. It didn't work, at least not immediately. It especially didn't work when Jack stretched toward her, took her chin gently between his fingers, and planted a firm, possessive kiss on her half-open mouth.

He leaned back in his chair then, nonchalantly sampling his drink as Eden struggled for composure. "What—what was that for?"

"Appearances," he said smoothly. "All part of the cover, Princess. Any complaints?"

"No. No, I guess not."

"Good," he said, and kissed her again.

Eden's jaw dropped in protest as she finally came up for air. "I can't believe you did that."

He merely grinned, apparently enjoying himself. "It's a tough job but somebody's got to do it."

"Speaking of jobs," she said, seething, "maybe you should be asking around about my missing fiancé instead of kissing me all the time!"

"Maybe. But the information the waitress just gave me wasn't half as fascinating as keeping up our cover."

"What information?"

"She's seen him."

"Armand? Where? When?"

"Right here, just a few nights ago."

"Here? So the farmer was right, then. But why didn't the front desk have any record of him?"

He shrugged. "Could be he used an AKA."

"You mean an alias? He wouldn't."

"Ed," he said gently, "you didn't believe he'd come here at all, but apparently he did. For all we know, he might still be here."

Eden cast a slightly guilty glance around the room. Armand here? As much as she wanted to find her fiancé, the thought of him walking in and seeing her with Jack made her feel as if she'd betrayed him somehow. Of course, her guilt was completely unfounded. She hadn't done anything that he wouldn't have completely approved of.

Okay, except for the kiss. Correction, three kisses. Not to mention the fact that she was parading around in an outfit that would make a French showgirl blush. No, Armand would never, never approve.

"What's wrong?" Jack asked.

"Nothing. Oh, I don't know. This doesn't seem right somehow. Dressing up. Stepping out on the town. Almost enjoying it."

"Almost?"

"Okay, enjoying it."

"So, you'd feel better if you were miserable?"

"Much," she said. "I shouldn't even be here."

"Ed, did it ever occur to you that it's Herman who should never have set foot in this place?"

No, actually it hadn't. But now that the question was out there, she couldn't help wondering how her sensible, scientific Armand had wound up in such a spot. How, or *why*.

"Whatever the reason," she said, thinking out loud, "I'm sure *he* didn't enjoy himself."

"Don't be so certain, Princess. You still haven't seen the floor show."

"There's a show? Do we have to stay for it? I mean, shouldn't we be leaving now?"

"Before all the fun begins?" he asked. "I don't think so. Especially not since we have a hot lead. There's a dancer I still need to talk to. According to the waitress, she might be able to tell us more about Armand. She's a twenty-something redhead. Goes by the name of Snake Woman."

"You've got to be kidding."

"Nope. The waitress promised that when the dancing started, I'd be able to spot her straight off."

Downing the rest of her drink, Eden reached for another one from a nearby tray. A dancer named Snake Woman? She couldn't imagine how that would be too hard to miss. What kind of weird floor show was this, anyway?

True to the waitress's prediction, as soon as the entertainment started, Snake Woman was among the easiest to spot. She didn't so much walk as *undulate* herself out into the center of the room as the music began to resonate with a whole new energy. The drums rolled, the spotlights focused, and the barely clad redhead writhed and slithered to the percussive sounds. As far as Eden's limited experience went with such things, it all seemed like fairly standard nightclub stuff. That is, until two large men in loincloths materialized from the mist and draped a ten-foot snake across the dancer's slender shoulders.

The men disappeared again, leaving Snake Woman to go it alone with only that long, ornately patterned python for a partner. The two of them twirled and twisted to the jungle music, gracefully entwining their bodies together until it was difficult to tell where one began and the other ended.

Just as Eden was getting used to the Snake Woman's primal ballet, acts two and three of the floor show began as two more dancers made their way to the spotlights at opposite ends of the room. One woman was adorned with a Vegas-style outfit, a gleaming white bikini trimmed lavishly with rhinestones. It was her headpiece, however, that was the real eye-catcher. Tall and exotic, it sprouted fan-shaped from her head in an arrangement of pure white feathers. Feathers that moved in unexpected ways as she strutted her stuff.

On second glance Eden realized that the headdress wasn't really a costume at all, but a pair of large, living birds that were balancing on the dancer's head, fanning their wide, white wings in display. Tropical cockatoos to be exact. Remarkably well-trained cockatoos.

A bright flash of brilliance from the other side of the room suddenly caught Eden's attention, and she turned to see what the third dancer was up to. This one was dressed like a butterfly in a form-fitting dark bodysuit, and the wings of her costume shimmered with iridescence as she moved.

The crowd clapped enthusiastically as the show gradually wound down. The dancers dispersed themselves among the tables, giving any interested audience members a chance to take a closer look. When Snake Woman and her unusual pet started rippling toward them, Jack motioned them over, deftly flashing a twenty-dollar bill between his fingers. Full-strength snake bait couldn't have worked any better or had a more instantaneous effect. Dancing faster and more suggestively than they had before, the two slithered up to their table at lightning speed.

From the moment the redhead arrived and began insinuating her svelte, incredibly supple body up against Jack, it was hard to tell just who was charming who. The dancer's bare leg found its way around Jack's waist in a movement that would've scored a perfect ten at a gymnastics meet. In appreciation for her outstanding efforts, he tucked the bill into the wriggling bottom of her bikini costume. A bikini so tight it was remarkable that there was any room available for such a generous tip.

"What do you think you're doing?" Eden whispered to Jack as the dancer continued to stretch and slink, twisting herself into strange contortions which were no doubt calculated to squeeze further cash from her intended victim.

"Just greasing the wheel," he said, smiling up at the dancer's smooth maneuvers with a look of speculative male interest that made Eden's stomach knot. "There's no such thing as free information. Besides, don't you think she deserves some sort of reward? Probably took years of training to learn how to move like that."

"Maybe it's just raw talent," she muttered sarcastically.

Really. It was bad enough to have to sit here and

watch the dancer ply her wicked ways with Jack's all-too-willing body, but to have him pay for the privilege out of *her* expense account was a bit too annoying to overlook. Okay, so he might be bribing the woman in hopes of getting more information out of her, but he didn't have to be enjoying himself in the process, did he?

A second, even bigger bill found its way into Snake Woman's overstretched costume.

"Hey!" Eden exclaimed bitterly. "That's a fifty she's flaunting there and we still haven't heard a single useful word out of her."

Apparently overhearing her impulsive complaint, the dancer laughed, turning her attentions full force on Jack. "Girlfriend always this uptight, is she?"

"Yeah," Jack said, in that languid drawl of his, "but it's not her fault. She just can't seem to help herself."

That was it, Eden decided. Murmuring a curt "Excuse me," she stood from her chair and headed for the nearest rest room.

Uptight? she seethed silently. *Can't help herself?* Of all the nerve. If the comments had been less believable, maybe they wouldn't have stung so much. If she hadn't downed that second, deceptively innocuous-tasting drink, it might've been clearer whether Jack had actually meant them or was simply schmoozing to get Snake Woman to trust him. Still, the words had hurt, possibly because she recognized the ring of truth in them.

Uptight? So what if she was? She preferred to think of herself as cautious. Careful. Responsible. All admirable character traits for any sane adult to possess in this day and age. So why didn't she admire them in herself?

Wobbling her way into the ladies' room on slightly shaky legs, she paused in front of the mirror.

Since when had she gotten so good at hiding how she felt, even from herself? Maybe it had something to do with a feeling so new to her, she barely even recognized the signs when they were staring her in the face. Her face. It wasn't anger that had made her leave the table in such a huff, but a raw, human reaction that was even simpler than that, more revealing.

Jealousy.

It had hit her suddenly, tearing at her insides with a pain so sharp, she could barely watch Snake Woman touching Jack. Tempting him, teasing him, writhing and wriggling against him with an enthusiasm that made Eden want to slap the dancer silly for her blatantly suggestive behavior. She hoped that affectionate trained snake of hers gave her a hard hug and a squeeze she would never forget.

As for her own behavior, how could she explain it? It wasn't at all like her to grow suddenly hostile toward a perfect stranger for no good reason. No good reason but one. The way she was starting to feel toward Jack Rafferty.

Dashing a few drops of cool water across her face, Eden did her best to tamp those feelings down again. Now was not the time to explore them. She wasn't sure she ever wanted to explore them.

Summoning her intestinal fortitude again, she exited the rest room, intending to return to the table and try to take whatever Snake Woman dished out with a little more grace and aplomb. But the show, apparently, was already over, and the crowd had swelled to impassable proportions as the clientele swarmed the floor to dance. The music rose by several decibels as the mass of swaying, gyrating patrons grew more raucous by the minute.

Standing on tiptoe as she scanned the crowd, Eden spotted Jack across the room. Alone, thank heavens. That awful woman had left. She started to make her way toward him, but a man in a suit stepped in front of her.

His cream linen jacket and pants were slightly wrinkled from humidity, but expensive in an obvious way. A gold watch and chain completed the outfit, standing out against his suntanned skin like cheap gilding on thick brown leather.

"Dance, lady?" he asked, and dragged her out onto the floor without bothering to wait for a response.

"What? Wait. No, thank you," she said firmly, but the music effectively drowned her out as her gorilla-sized partner grinned down at her, unheeding. "Are you *listening* to me?" she shouted as he took her by the shoulders and pressed his weight lifter's body against hers.

It quickly became apparent to her that the man was intoxicated. She could have easily detected the rum on his breath from ten feet away. Unfortunately, she was a little closer than that at the moment. But it was even more apparent to her that any form of protest was an exercise in futility at this point. Apart from coming down hard on Gorilla Guy's toes with the sharp heel of her sandal, there was little she could do to get his attention. The simplest course of action would be to go along with the dance and make a dash to leave the moment it was over.

"Don't be so uptight, baby," he told her as she woodenly followed his rocking, gyrating lead. "Loosen up a little."

Uptight? There was that word again! Eden bristled defensively at the sound of it. It reminded her there was nothing she would like more than to prove to Jack Rafferty that it didn't apply to her. Shaking her stuff with Gorilla Guy here could be the perfect opportunity.

"Loosen up? I'm liquid," she promised, lifting her chin, "just watch me."

SEVEN

The boast she'd made was reckless, Eden realized, but Gorilla Guy's response to it was encouraging. Maybe too encouraging, as he quickly became emboldened by her impulsive words. His huge hands slipped from her shoulders to her hips as he bumped their bodies together below the waist, rotating his pelvis in a dirty-dancing move that would've made the rock'n'roll King himself proud.

"Oomph!" Eden exclaimed as the sudden grinding startled the wind right out of her. Goodness, but what the man lacked in sheer style he certainly made up for in enthusiasm.

"Shake it, baby." He grabbed hold of her wrist and whirled her away from him in a wild piroutte, then quickly reeled her in again, yo-yo style.

Shake it? Was this guy stuck in the Saturday night disco seventies, or what? Besides, he wasn't giving her a chance to shake anything. He was too busy churning and vibrating and joggling her thoroughly himself.

"Get a grip on reality, bud-d-d-d-dy," she stuttered,

her voice vibrating in time with the involuntary bouncing of her body. "I am n-n-n-not your ba-a-a-by!"

But Gorilla seemed to have gone deaf again as his hips locked once more with hers, palpitating and pulsating with crude male movements. The gold chain on his chest shimmied wildly from the motion as the dark hair beneath it grew damp and sheened with sweat.

"Owooo!" he yelped wolfishly, working himself fast into a heated frenzy. "Wild thing!"

"That's *it*," Eden said, instinctively recoiling. With open palms to Gorilla's grossly gleaming torso, she tried to push herself away.

"No way, baby." He clamped his hands down hard on her arms and held her fast. "You're not going anywhere."

"Wanna bet?" she asked, and brought a bent knee upward, making sharp, insistent contact with his groin. Unfortunately, the move wasn't half as effective as the few times she'd practiced it in self-defense class. Instead of bringing Gorilla Guy instantly to his knees, he jerked back only slightly, as if he'd been stung by an annoying insect.

"Like I said, lady," he said, growling angrily, "you're not going anywhere. Unless it's back to my bungalow."

A sickening sense of fear began to rise inside her throat. He was serious, she realized. At first she'd thought he was too loose and intoxicated to be a real threat. Now she understood he was just drunk enough to be dangerous.

"No chance of that," she said, and tried again to free herself, struggling fiercely to snatch her hands away.

To her horror, his grip on her only grew tighter. Worse, she felt herself being dragged, rag-doll-style, toward the nightclub door. A scream rose inside her, but before the sound had a chance to come out, Gorilla Guy suddenly let go. Astonished, she watched as his huge head jerked backward, caught at the collar by some savage, unseen force.

A split second later he was whipped around where he stood and lifted almost off his feet. A noise resonated, the awful sound of a fist striking hard against flesh, and Gorilla Guy's head snapped back again from the force of it. He wobbled for a moment, swaying to and fro in a stunned state of shock, then finally toppled, facedown on the floor.

It was only after she watched the creep fall and his bulky body no longer blocked her view, that Eden got a good look at his attacker. Jack Rafferty. Correction, a very angry Jack Rafferty. His chest was heaving, his jaw muscles working, his green eyes blazing with open fury.

Fury not only at the man he'd just decked, but at *her*.

With a final glance down at his unfortunate victim, who was starting to regain consciousness, he grabbed her by the wrist and pulled her back toward the door, grimly clearing a way for them through the crowd.

"Move it, Ed," he said, barking at her roughly. "Let's get out of here."

Some fine rescuer he was. He was acting every bit as obnoxious and domineering as the sicko in the cream suit, manhandling her all the way back to their bungalow. He'd saved her all right, that much was certain, but who was going to save her from him?

The bungalow door slammed shut behind them and he turned to her, his expression rife with barely controlled anger.

"What the hell did you think you were doing back

there?" he demanded, his voice hard and lethal, deceptively low.

"Dancing," she managed to say calmly, casting a concerned glance at Babette, who was watching them, wide-eyed, from a pillow in the corner. Normally the poodle rushed to greet her immediately, but the sound of the door had startled her. Jack's tone, too, had probably put her off from any immediate displays of affection. The little dog seemed to sense it was time to hold back.

"You're scaring her," Eden added, pointing to the poodle.

"I don't think so," he said smoothly. "At least *she* has the good sense to stay put when it's prudent, which is more than I can say for you."

"Excuse me," she said indignantly, "for not being more obedient. Maybe you'd like me to wear a leash and collar too."

"It would sure make you easier to handle."

"I didn't hire you to *handle* me. Although you've been doing a pretty thorough job of it so far."

"No doubt you'd prefer Muscleman's touch to mine," he said cruelly.

"I—no, of course not. That's not what I meant. I——thank you for stepping in when you did. I appreciate it."

"Could've fooled me. Ed, what the devil possessed you to provoke a man like that?"

"I didn't provoke him! All I did was dance. Jeez, is there some law against that that I'm not aware of?"

"What you're not aware of is the kind of risk you took. The position you put yourself in."

"By dancing? Did I miss something here?"

"Princess, you have no idea what a dangerous place the world really is. What can happen to a woman all alone. Unprotected . . ."

Eden stared at him, puzzled. Apparently she *had* missed something. Either that, or what Jack was saying just didn't make sense. It wasn't her fault that some inebriated nightclub patron had tried to step over the line. The situation had escalated beyond her control, and while it had been serious, it seemed that Jack's anger with her was slightly misplaced.

"Look, Rafferty, don't you think you're overreacting a little? I did survive after all, thanks to you."

"You were lucky," he said bluntly. "Some people aren't."

"Some people? People such as . . . ?"

He hesitated for a long time, disconcerted by her question. "Such as someone I once knew," he finally responded, albeit reluctantly. "Someone I wasn't there to protect."

"A friend of yours?" she prompted.

"A relative," he said. "My little sister. Lara."

Eden swallowed hard at the catch she heard in his voice, a tone that told her his pain was excruciating. Whomever he was angry at, she was starting to understand it wasn't her. He'd never mentioned his sister before. His father, she knew, had not been loving, but the affection with which he mentioned Lara's name was clear. As deep as the ache that seemed to be behind it.

"Tell me about it," she said gently, and took him by the hand, leading him to the edge of the bed and settling down beside him.

The story he related came slowly at first, in short, clipped words and sketchy details, but gradually he pieced the picture together for her from years before. Fifteen years to be exact, a long time for anyone to keep their pain buried inside them. Too long to continue searching and hunting for a lost little girl with small odds of finding her and even smaller odds of obtaining any personal relief.

If there was anything Eden learned about Jack from the tale he told her, it was this: He'd never stopped searching for Lara. Never given up on her. But neither had he given himself a chance to grieve.

He'd been fighting his emotions for years on end, refusing to face them for fear they might hamper his ability to keep going. Acknowledging his grief was tantamount to acknowledging that his sister was lost forever. And no matter how high the likelihood of that was, he refused to give in to reality. Or to let go of his own guilt for what had happened to her.

Lord, no wonder he was still in so much pain, even after all this time. It was a palpable thing that surrounded him constantly, hanging in the air between them. Eden could feel it gnawing away at him like some virulent, burning acid, gradually eating its way through every steel wall of self-defense he'd tried to erect against it. His suffering had been slow and exquisite.

Sensitive and empathetic since her secluded childhood, Eden was far more in tune to emotions than most. More in tune to distress of any sort. It was the reason she'd had to save Babette from being cruelly caged, as well as the carefully considered rationale behind her current search for Armand. She was looking for him not simply because he was her fiancé, but because if someone she knew was in serious trouble, she wanted to help.

Was that why Jack Rafferty had opened himself up to her, if only for a moment? Because he knew she would be able to understand? Or was it just possible that his temporary trust in her meant something more?

Pushing the stray thought to the back of her head, she tried to concentrate on helping Jack somehow, if only by relieving him in some small way. "You feel guilty about Lara, don't you?" she asked.

The laugh he gave her was harsh, bitter. Just from the sound of it Eden understood whom he was angriest at.

Himself.

"Princess," he said, "I wrote the book on the subject. Why shouldn't I feel guilty when it's my fault she disappeared?"

"How can you be so certain of that when you don't know what really happened to her? Maybe things would've turned out exactly the same if you'd been living at home at the time."

"No," he insisted, swearing harshly. "I might've done something to stop it. God, at least I should have been there to look out for her when I knew how worthless my parents were. Dammit, I *knew*."

"But your parents were divorced by the time you left for college, weren't they? Your father wasn't around then much, was he?"

"Hell, he wasn't around much when they were married. But he did have visiting privileges to see her, not that he used them very often. Once every few months, maybe. After she disappeared, there was no reason for him to come around at all."

"So you thought Lara was safe with your mother when you took off. Leaving your little sister with her maternal parent is hardly a reckless act on your part."

"Safe is a relative term," he said. "My mom's drinking got worse after the divorce."

"I still don't see what you could have done."

"I could have stayed at home where I was needed instead of trying to get myself through college. I should have known that a Rafferty trying to make something better of himself was flying in the face of fate. I just didn't want to own up to the fact that I would always be my father's son, no matter how hard I tried to get away from it."

"So you should have put your life on hold and just hung around waiting for Lara to grow up?"

"Exactly."

"Jack, no one would expect that of you. She was your little sister, not your child."

"Hell, Ed," he whispered hoarsely. "I loved her."

"I know."

Eden's throat constricted with emotion as she watched him trying to handle the feeling. Love. To Jack, the whole meaning of that word revolved around an ever present ache in his life. And his heart.

She would give almost anything at the moment to try to alleviate that ache inside him. He was flexing the fingers of his right hand absently, testing the same muscles he'd used to save her from the gorilla in the nightclub. Glancing down at the back of that hand, Eden realized his knuckles were bleeding. He'd cut himself, painfully splitting his flesh open in the process of punching that creep out.

Instinctively she reached out to comfort him there, covering his wounded fingers with her own.

"Does it hurt?" she asked.

His gaze lifted, locked with hers, beautiful and blazing with a hot, green fire. "Don't do that."

"Please let me," she whispered. "I want to."

"Want to what, Princess? Comfort me? Kiss the hurt away?"

"Yes, that."

"Sorry," he said, gently removing her trembling fingers. "Touching in private is against the rules, remember?"

"I don't care," she said, and lifted the hand he'd injured doing battle for her, bringing it to her lips to kiss the wounded spot.

"Ed, have mercy on me."

"What do you think I'm doing?"

"Woman," he said, his hand moving slowly across her face, caressing her cheeks, her temples, her mouth. His fingertips were callused, slightly rough and scratchy, but his touch was soft and warm, amazingly gentle for a man of his size. "Do you have any idea what you're doing to me?"

No, actually, she didn't. She only knew that she felt a yearning well from somewhere deep inside her, so fierce it left her breathless.

"Tell me," she said, her voice soft and shaky.

He pulled back to study her, still looking deep into her eyes. "Where should I start, Princess?" he asked her huskily. "Maybe here." He reached around the back of her hair to pull the pins free of their confining hold. The dark strands loosened and fell, spilling over onto his hands. He caught them between his fingers, touching and stroking as if her hair itself was as fine and costly as the rarest silk.

"This," he said, "makes me crazy. Crazy to touch it. To feel it. Sink my hands into it."

Eden's breath caught. She didn't dare speak. She couldn't.

He ducked his head to her throat, grazing his mouth against the bare skin of her neck, working his way upward until he found a particularly tender, trembling spot. The spot where her pulse was pounding wildly for him. His lips brushed against it, sampling, exploring.

"This," he went on, talking low and languidly as the slow, excruciating journey continued, "makes me want you. Your skin. Your scent. The way your heart beats faster whenever I'm close."

A shaky sigh escaped her. Lord, but his technique was exquisite torture. Sweet torture.

His mouth moved higher. He took the lobe of her ear between his teeth, nipping lightly against the sensitive, nerve-rich area. Eden gasped at the shocking pleasure of it.

"That," he groaned, whispering softly against the open orifice, "makes me hot. The way you respond to the slightest things I do. Little things, like this . . ." His tongue darted inside the opening, making a slow, moist circle around the tingling inner rim of her ear.

The moan Eden made was so delicate, it was almost a whimper.

"God, yes," Jack said, breathing hard, "you do make me hot."

Closing her eyes, she clutched the edge of the bed, trying to ground herself again in reality. It wasn't any use. She couldn't believe the things he was saying. She couldn't believe the way they made her feel.

"Now," he said, "I've told you exactly what you do to me. Now will you let me show you?"

She opened her eyes again, her lashes fluttering wide as she struggled to find her voice. "Show me?" She could only imagine what he meant by that. Her face flushed wildly at the thought of it.

"I'll take that as a yes," he said, "until you want me to stop. Just say when, Princess."

He paused to pull his jacket off, tossing it nonchalantly onto the floor. The cotton shirt came off next, quickly following the sport coat. Eden swallowed hard, a quick jolt of fear leaping suddenly to her throat. If he reached for the top button of those blue jeans, she swore she was going to make a quick dash for the door.

He didn't.

He reached for her hand instead and placed it palm-open across his bare chest. She felt his heart beating very fast beneath it. Eden's own heart squeezed tight in response. On some level, he was trying to show her how vulnerable he was to her nearness.

Almost as vulnerable as she was to him.

He drew her hand down, slowly, until her fingertips grazed firmly against several sets of stony muscles. The broad curve of his pectorals, as tan and steely as if they had been cast from molten metal. The tightly toned ripples of his abs. The muscle below his belt, the hardest one of all, rigidly erect and totally male.

Eden's eyes widened when she felt him there. Gracious, he was incredibly aroused. She could barely believe how huge and beautifully hard he was. Was that what she did to him?

Jack winced with sweet torment when she finally touched him there. The pleasure she brought him was so soaring and sharp, it was almost pain. Shyly her fingers explored the length of him, fluttering timidly as she determined for herself the full extent of his arousal. Her touch was timid, butterfly-light, but so amazingly innocent, she had him in agony in seconds.

Shuddering, he caught her by the wrist. "You're pushing my limits, Princess. There's only so much temptation a man can take before he needs to do something about it."

Temptation? That had to be the understatement of the year, Jack decided. In truth, she was driving him wild.

"Oh!" she said. "Are you going to do something about it?"

Damn straight, he decided, and caught her other wrist in his hand, capturing both of her arms over her head. "Yes." He covered her mouth with his own.

They fell back on the bed together, caught up in the kiss, as his lips settled against hers. Angling his head, he teased her mouth apart with his tongue, then plunged it deep inside her. Muscles fisted hard down below as he sampled her wetness with a hunger he'd never known before. But a single kiss, no matter how explosive, wouldn't be enough to satisfy him this time.

There were too many other parts of her he was determined to explore. Lord, he wanted to taste every sweet inch of this woman. His ministrations moved from her mouth to the tops of her eyelids, which were closed and trembling. He kissed each one, then the tip of her nose, the nape of her neck, the cleft of her throat where the low-cut dress revealed a soft vee of sensual skin.

Not quite enough skin, as far as Jack was concerned. Her breasts rose and fell beneath the thin covering of silk, inciting him to investigate further. Still holding her arms captive with one of his hands, he turned his attention to the soft twin mounds, experimentally running his palm across them. Ed moaned as the peaks pebbled tightly from his touch.

Jack groaned inwardly, grateful that she wasn't wearing a bra. Did she have any idea just how sexy that was? It quickly became a personal mission to show her. With the insubstantial fabric still hiding her from his view, he took one swollen center between the tips of his fingers and massaged it thoroughly.

Ed twisted beneath him, whimpering with pleasure.

The tip he was touching grew more turgid and tender with every light, grinding movement he made. Fascinated, Jack flicked his thumb across it and was rewarded with a sweet, agonized groan.

Those little sounds she gave made him hot, exciting him beyond belief. He could take her right now if he wanted to. She was so needy already, he doubted she'd protest at all. Only that wasn't the way he wanted it between them. He didn't simply want her to accept what he did. He wanted her to welcome it openly.

Hell, he wanted her to beg for him.

And then he planned to give her so much pleasure, it would obliterate Herman from her mind forever.

Still massaging her between his fingers, he continued until she was gasping for relief. Even then he didn't stop. He moved his hand to the other inviting mound, took the bud between his fingers, and began the sweet torture all over again.

As the level of his own excitement rose with hers, the urge to feel more of her mounted. To see more of her. Reaching behind, he released the snap on her dress and tugged the shimmering fabric to her waist in a single, swift movement. Both breasts were bare before him.

Ed glanced away from him, too self-conscious to meet his gaze, but Jack did his best to reassure her.

"Princess," he said hoarsely, "you're beautiful."

So beautiful, he couldn't stop himself from taking one dusky nipple into his mouth and suckling until Ed's back arched off the bed.

"Jack," she cried softly, "it's too much."

He stopped for a second, soothing her with his words. "Settle down, baby, I'm just getting started."

Taking the wet, pink tip to himself again, Jack sipped and tugged, pulling and circling the peak with his lips, drinking her in until he was intoxicated from the taste of her. High, but still not satiated.

There was so much more he wanted to do with her. More he needed to do. Starting with the second breast. Tracing his tongue along the outer edges of the overflowing mound, he worked his way inward in ever narrowing circles, teasing but never touching the hard, budding center. Never tasting the peak where he knew she ached for him to assuage her.

"Lord," Ed said. "I don't think I can take this."

Jack had to admit he was in pretty rough shape himself. No, he was in hard shape, to be exact. Stiff enough to break rocks.

"No?" he whispered back, smiling wickedly. "Let's see if you can take this."

Eden waited in shivering suspense as she wondered what Jack was going to do next. She was close to pleading with him by now, she knew. But pleading for what, she wasn't sure. To stop? To go on? Was it possible to want both of those things all at once?

A few moments earlier she hadn't thought it possible that she could feel this kind of burning desire. Now she wasn't sure she could survive it. If he didn't touch her soon, she wasn't sure if she could live without it.

He did touch her, finally. He tasted her exquisitely, taking her nipple into his mouth and lathing it fully with his tongue. So fully that Eden thought she would scream from the slow, stroking pleasure of it. Just when she thought she would die from the feeling, he drew back, studying the dampness that still clung to the center of both breasts. Tenderly he bent his head again and blew air across the lingering wetness.

It was one of the most erotic feelings she had ever known, soothing and sensual at once. But just when she was starting to catch her breath again, Jack's hands moved to her waist and pushed her dress down past her hips, past her thighs until it pooled into a dark, silken pile at her feet. She lay before him, naked to the waist, wearing nothing but her panties, garter belt, and lace-topped stockings of the finest French silk.

Instinctively her hands went to her own exposed body, shyly attempting to cover herself.

"Don't, Princess," he said. "You're so perfect. Let me look at you."

Look at her? she wondered. He was practically devouring her with his hot, green gaze. Ravenous, that's what Jack Rafferty's appetite was. His hunger emanated not only from his eyes but from his hands as well. All at once they were caressing her legs from the hollows of her ankles to the curves of her calves, the tops of her thighs and higher.

Smoothly he unsnapped the hooks that secured her right stocking. At the direction of his hand, the silk whispered down, snaking its way toward her ankle until her leg was bare. The left stocking followed shortly. Seconds later his hands were all over the smooth, naked stretch of skin he'd just exposed.

Gradually he made his way up her legs, stopping momentarily to focus his attention on certain areas.

Merciless, he continued along the deliciously dangerous path until his attention was focused on the uppermost cleft of her thighs. His hands delved between them, parting her legs. Her heart shot straight to her throat.

His fingertips teased, toying with the edge of her panties.

Eden could swear her heart stopped. Stopped and then started again as it went a little crazy. Was he really going to touch her *there*? In that throbbing spot where she yearned for him the most, ached for him with all of her being?

"Please," she whispered, wild with wanting, yet terrified of the havoc he was wreaking within her. "Please, Jack. Don't."

She heard him swear softly, breathing hard. His hands froze in mid-motion, gently withdrew. "Princess," he said, not unkindly, "you're killing me."

"Trust me," she said, "the feeling is mutual."

"What is it, then?" he asked, far more patiently than she might've expected under the circumstances.

"It's—me," she said, her arm over her face as she tried to shield herself from the shame she was feeling. Shame for the excitement she should never have allowed herself to experience in the first place. "I can't."

"Can't?" he repeated quietly. "Ed, I think you're fooling yourself. It's pretty clear you want to."

It was true. She did want to. Lord, how she wanted to. There was no arguing with the obvious truth or with the fact that she'd let Jack seduce her this far.

"You don't understand," she said, sitting up, pulling the bedcovers protectively around her.

Jack shifted his position and leaned back against the bedboard, raking a shock of hair from his eyes. "Try me."

He looked so sexy sitting there in his bare chest and blue jeans that Eden wasn't sure she had the strength to tell him what she needed to. Could she share her innermost secrets with him and still survive emotionally? Somehow the prospect of revealing her physical shortcomings was less frightening than having him discover them for himself. What she had to say was difficult to talk about under any circumstances. Could she trust Jack to tread lightly?

There was only one sure way to find out.

"For starters," she said, "I can't do this to Armand. I can't betray him."

Jack's eyebrows arched. "Betray him? Last time I looked, there was no wedding ring on your hand. Come to think of it, Ed, your engagement ring hasn't been there lately either."

"I only took it off temporarily," she said, "for safe-keeping."

"Oh?"

"Don't say it like that! It's true."

"Okay, it's true. But the fact remains, you're not married."

"No," she agreed, "I'm not. But even if I was prepared to go back on my promise to Armand, I can't. Physically, I mean. I really *can't.*"

He shook his head, clearly confused. "Come back with that again, Princess. What are you saying? That you're . . ."

"Frigid," she supplied bluntly. "I'm frigid, all right? Incapable of experiencing a sexual climax."

For nearly a minute Jack fell silent, seeming to consider the information she'd given him. She felt decidedly sick to her stomach as she waited for some sort of response. If he turned away from her in loathing or disgust, she wasn't sure she could handle it. She wouldn't blame him for steering clear. It was a condition many men would be intimidated by.

Especially virile, decidedly macho men like Jack. Judging by his amazing skill, he was clearly experienced in bed. Experienced? He was a master where women were concerned. Probably had to beat them off with a whip.

How would a guy like that deal with a woman who was all but impervious to his ultimate charms? A woman who couldn't be satisfied. She might not be so experienced in sexual matters, but she knew enough to understand how a man might feel about that. Threatened to the very core of his masculinity.

And while Jack was certainly more masculine than most men, Eden wasn't sure how he would react. She cared enough about his opinion to pray he wouldn't lose his respect for her.

He didn't, thank goodness.

He took her in his arms and hugged her instead, gently stroking her hair and shoulders as if she were a child in need of reassurance. Eden's heart squeezed tight at the gesture. It was exactly what she needed at the moment, and one of the most comforting acts of kindness she had ever known.

He didn't despise her. Didn't turn away and want to wash his hands of her. But he also didn't seem to believe her.

"Princess," he said, pulling back to look at her. "I promise you that's not possible. You're too sexy. Too responsive."

"To a point," she explained. "But then there's a line I'm unable to cross. Trust me, I've tried. I just can't."

"I do trust you, Ed. But have you ever considered the possibility that it's not your problem but someone else's?"

"What are you saying? That it's Armand's fault?"

"I'm not talking about fault here. Maybe if you've had to try that hard, you've simply been trying with the wrong man."

She blinked up at him silently, ashamed to admit that the same disloyal thought had crossed her mind once or twice. What if it was Armand's problem, or rather a sign of some problem between the two of them? It was a possibility she just couldn't bring herself to consider. Certainly not now, while her fiancé was missing, maybe even in danger.

"Armand," she said stubbornly, "is not the wrong man."

Jack shook his head slowly. "Sure you want to bet your life on that, Ed? Because that's what we're talking about. Spending your entire life with someone who can never make you happy."

"And I suppose you think you can?"

"Princess," he said, taking her chin in his hand and forcing her to meet his gaze squarely. "If you'll let me, I can take you to paradise."

EIGHT

Trying to get some sleep while sprawled out on a bunch of blankets on the floor was hardly Jack's idea of paradise. But that was exactly where Ed had banished him to after making it clear she had no intention of following him there. To paradise, that is.

Or to the floor, for that matter.

While she was snoozing comfortably in the king-sized bed, he was fighting a serious case of insomnia. It wasn't that easy to sleep with a three-pound poodle curled up on your chest, but apparently Babette had taken a liking to him. Actually it was impossible to shake the little furball. She seemed to have gotten it into her canine mind that he was the dominant dog in their small social pack. From that point on, she'd been determined to sleep with him.

Too bad her mistress couldn't take a lesson from her and curl up on his chest instead. But unfortunately, no such luck. So much for the thought of Eden finding ecstasy in his arms. Correction, the *fantasy* of Eden. The woman was as elusive and off-limits as the garden she was named after.

As innocent too. So the lady had never been to
heaven and back, had she? It was a crying shame, as far
as Jack was concerned. Herman really ought to be
ashamed of himself. Eden certainly had no reason to be.

It was downright unfair for her to blame herself for
the lack of passion between herself and her missing fiancé.

Ms. Wellbourne was clearly *not* frigid. He'd felt her
respond to him all right and had felt himself responding
right back. Hell, she'd been so incredibly passionate,
they had already been halfway there by the time she'd
pulled back. He had no doubt he could take her all the
way if she would only let herself go with him.

Why wouldn't she let herself go?

For one thing, she'd spent the majority of her adult
life trying to do just the opposite. Trying to stop sensations from reaching her. Ed's senses were so finely
tuned and talented, she'd trained herself to block them
out in self-defense. If she ever opened herself up to
them again, the sensual explosion that followed would
probably rock them both to the core.

Jack wanted to be there when that happened. He
wanted to help her. But there was something else
preventing Ed from opening up the floodgates of her
feelings.

That something was named Herman. Or at least
the fairy-tale picture of what he represented. Prince
Charming. Happily-ever-after. A man who would stick
around the way her own father had not.

How in the hell was he supposed to compete with
that? Not with the real man, who was still suspiciously
absent, but with the distorted, all-too-perfect image Ed
had of him in her mind. He couldn't compete with it,
that was the problem.

Steadiness, security, commitment. If those were the qualities she was looking for in a man, he had none of the above to offer her. Zippo, zilch. Nada.

Never having had the chance or the inclination to settle down, he'd spent most of his adult life on the move. Maybe not out of personal choice at first, but surely it was too late to change all that, even if he wanted to. Was he even considering it? How could he when his life had never really been his own since the day of Lara's disappearance?

Why would he consider it now, after all these years? There was only one logical reason he could think of. Ms. Ed Wellbourne. In spite of his concerted efforts to prevent it, the woman was starting to get under his skin.

No, it was even worse than that. Feelings were starting to surface inside him at the thought of her. Feelings that went far beyond the sexual. *Those* he could handle just fine. It was the other kind that worried him. The ones that felt suspiciously like—aw hell—*emotions*.

Deadly, unlooked-for emotions.

For starters he was protective of her. Why else would he have all but broken a man's jaw to rescue her? A less obvious method would have been far more in keeping with his preferred, low-profile style. Instead, like a jealous idiot in a testosterone-induced rage, he'd attracted all sorts of unwanted attention toward them.

What the devil had come over him? It was a dangerous slip, one that could potentially affect the outcome of the case. Now, *that* was the most bothersome repercussion of all. He was starting to care just a little too much for this woman, in spite of the potential complications that caring might cause. He was starting to have feelings for her.

Feelings that were scaring the hell out of him.

It was nearly dawn when he heard the faint, scratching sound at the door. Turning toward it, he saw a single piece of paper being slipped under the threshold. Still bleary-eyed from lack of sleep, his first impression was that the front desk had sent over some sort of checkout bill. But a second glance told him the document just didn't look right to be a hotel tab.

The paper was too upscale and expensive looking, not the standard sort of computer-generated printout he'd expect. There was no logo on it either, at least not one distinctive enough to detect from his vantage point on the floor. To Jack's well-trained eye, those were signs enough to arouse suspicion.

Rolling onto his side, he deposited Babette onto the blanket, then leapt to his feet and made a dash for the door. Jerking it open with a force that made the hinges scream, he shot a 180-degree glance outside, searching for any sign of the unknown note-dropper. But whoever it was that had left the mysterious missive had already disappeared.

Still keeping an observant eye out from the open doorway, Jack bent to retrieve the letter. Skimming over the half page or so of neatly typed text, he whistled softly under his breath. Based on the contents of the few terse paragraphs, the stakes in the search for Herman had just been raised.

"What is it?" Ed asked, sitting up in bed.

"Bad news," he said bluntly.

Pushing back the covers, she quickly padded across the floor in bare feet and satin pajamas. "Tell me," she insisted, reaching his side. "Has something happened to him?"

"If this letter's to be believed," Jack said, handing her the paper, "he's been kidnapped."

Ed's face went white as she took it from him and carefully read what for all intents and purposes appeared to be a ransom note. Finishing the message, she looked up at him, shaking her head in confusion. "What are you saying? That you don't believe it?"

"I don't know, Ed. It just doesn't smell right. For starters, who delivered the thing?"

She cast another quick glance at the letter, or more specifically, at the stationery it was typed on. "I have no idea who left it," she told him, "but the paper looks exactly like what Scentsations uses, minus the logo. It's definitely their signature color."

Jack lifted his eyebrows at her. "So it fits with the corporate espionage theory? Or in this case, corporate kidnapping?"

"They're asking for the other half of the formula, aren't they? My half. Who else would want it?"

"More importantly," he speculated slowly, "who in the hell even knows that we're here?"

Eden stretched her arms wide. "Who *doesn't* know, after the scene in the nightclub last night? Maybe the waitress got the word around that we were looking for him. Or, what if Snake Woman kept talking after we left? To anyone who was interested. Maybe the kidnappers themselves were there."

"Maybe."

"What *did* Snake Woman have to say for herself, anyway? Did she remember seeing Armand?"

"Sure did. Sorry to have to tell you this, Ed, but it seems he showed up for the floor show several nights in a row."

"What? I don't believe it. Serpent Lady's brain must be oxygen deprived from one squeeze too many. Either that or she was tempted to lie at the sight of all those bills."

Jack shrugged, falling momentarily silent. There was no kind way to tell Ed he believed the dancer's version of events. Herman hadn't simply been hanging out around the club, he'd been enjoying himself. Ordering buckets of champagne, living high off the hog, dancing with anything that moved. Acting as if he'd been celebrating something. Either he'd been throwing himself a helluva bachelor party or . . .

"Did she have anything else to say?" Ed asked, breaking into his thoughts.

"That's as much as I got out of her."

"If we don't meet the demands in this letter, Armand won't live to see the wedding!"

Loyally reacting to the sound of her mistress in sudden distress, Babette bounded forward, jumping and barking as she sniffed and scratched at the threshold of the open door. Ed leaned down to try and comfort her, but the determined little dog would have none of it. Escaping her hold, she dashed for the doorway, stopped just a foot or so outside the bungalow, and barked, pawing frantically at the ground.

"Babette!" Ed called. "Come back here."

"No," Jack said softly, putting his hand up. "Hold on a second. Let's see what she does."

Fascinated by whatever scent she'd picked up on, the poodle continued to paw at the ground directly outside the door. Circling and yelping, she finally stopped, squatted, and relieved herself on the woven sisal doormat.

"What do you suppose that means?" Jack asked curiously, thinking out loud.

"It means she just spent six hours sleeping and had

to pee," Ed said in frustration, shooing Babette inside again and closing the door behind them.

"You think that's all there is to it?"

"Of course. Now, do you mind if we get back to more serious matters? The note, for instance."

"Right. The note. Guess we'd better decide exactly what we're going to do about it."

Ed sank back onto the bed, looking so downright despondent, it was all Jack could do to stop himself from going to her and slowly soothing all her worries away.

"I don't see what we can do except comply," she said, holding her head in her hands. "They're threatening to kill Armand if I don't hand over my half of the formula."

He folded his arms across his chest, pacing back and forth across the room as he tried to make some sense of the situation. "I hate to point this out, Ed, but there's no guarantee he won't be killed even if you do turn it over. I don't like the delivery method. They want you to send it over the Internet, right? Via e-mail. Sounds way too slippery to me. An electronic ransom response is going to make the bad guys almost impossible to trace."

But it wasn't only the delivery instructions that were making Jack extremely suspicious. It seemed to him there were too many hints as to the possible identity of the kidnappers. In his experience the bad guys usually didn't try so hard to give themselves away.

In this case all the clues pointed straight to some thugs who'd been hired by a rival perfume house. Pointed just a little too clearly for comfort, making him wonder exactly who had authored the note. Corporate French crooks? Maybe. But then again, maybe not.

Either way, a carefully planned response was required. One that fell short of simply handing over the formula, but still managed not to risk Herman's life. Hell, he wasn't going to let the bastard die if he could help it. The only way Ed was ever going to sort her feelings out was if they found the guy in one piece.

"There must be some method," he said, thinking out loud, "that would make it necessary to deliver what they want in person instead of electronically. At least that would give Herman his best chance of surviving this. We don't hand over the goods until we see him for ourselves. That is, assuming you're willing to hand over the goods in exchange for him."

"Of course I am!" she said, firing up in anger.

Jack watched in fascination as her eyebrows lifted with attitude. Her eyes flashed, her nostrils flared, but it was the way her chin lifted in stubborn defiance that really got to him. Desire tugged deep in his belly. He loved it when she got riled. He'd never seen anything sexier.

"Just checking," he said, resisting the urge to push her back on the bed and finish what they'd started last night. "We're not talking about peanuts here, Ed. Based on what you told me, that formula's worth millions. Mucho millions, right? I hope Herman's worth it."

She folded her arms across her chest, more incensed than ever. "I'm not even going to dignify that with an answer."

"Fine. Then get your brain busy working on an answer to our little problem instead. What to use as a more tangible form of bait to lure the kidnappers in with."

"That's simple," she said, surprising him. "I know the perfect thing. Not the written formula, but the perfume itself."

"The perfume? Wait a second, Ed, I thought this stuff was so new it wasn't even being manufactured yet."

"It isn't, but I still have a small sample of it from the prototype batch the lab scientists put together. It was a present from Armand. A memento of all the hard work we'd done together."

"How romantic," he commented dryly.

"It was," she said wistfully. "He gave it to me on our first date."

"I think I'm going to lose my breakfast."

"You haven't had any breakfast," Ed reminded him.

"Oh, yeah. Nevertheless, maybe you'd better explain why the 'nappers would be willing to accept a sample when they're looking for the whole recipe."

"That's easy. With just a few drops of the original scent, they can chemically analyze the ingredients and figure out the formula for themselves."

"Ed," Jack said, "you're a genius."

"Thank you."

"So where is it?"

"The perfume? Back at the shop."

"So what are you waiting for, Princess? Let's get packed up and get out of here. We've got work to do."

They were back in Jack's houseboat again before Eden had a clear picture of their immediate plan. The luggage had been loaded, but instead of making a move to cast off and head back for Winter Park, Jack took a seat in his desk chair, settling himself in front of the computer screen.

"What are you doing?" she asked him. "I thought we were going straight to the shop."

"We are," he assured her, flipping on the master

switch that powered up the machine's battery pack, "but not just yet." He pulled the ransom note from the front pocket of his shirt and reread the e-mail address they'd been instructed to send the formula to. "I want to get a message off to our friendly kidnappers first. Tell them about our little change of plan and hope they swallow the bait. If nothing else, the ploy should buy us some time."

The screen glowed to life, displaying a series of software icons. Jack scrolled through them quickly, selecting a program that would link the computer straight to the Internet via cell phone modem. Seconds later he was composing a curt electronic letter, suggesting the crooks would be wise to satisfy themselves with a sample of the perfume itself instead of the written recipe.

Eden pushed a pile of papers to one side of the desk, then perched herself on the cleared-off edge and watched Jack's tersely typed words marching rapidly across the screen.

"Care to proof it?" he asked.

She shook her head. "Sounds fine to me."

"Good. Hand me a disk, then, would you?" He indicated a small plastic storage box on the desk beside her. "I want to back this up with a copy, just in case."

Eden rifled through the container. Settling on the only diskette that appeared to be blank, she handed it to him.

Jack inserted it smoothly into the A drive and glanced up at her. "Your shop's computer is on-line, isn't it?"

She wrinkled her forehead, trying to remember what Hope had told her about her recent efforts to update their system. "We don't have a fully constructed Web site yet. So far, we're only set up to send and receive e-mail."

"That's enough for our purposes. What's the address?"

She told him, briefly reciting the short sequence of letters as he entered them into the keyboard. "Why not just give your address?" she asked.

"Simple. We're not going to have access to this machine for much longer. We're leaving it behind as soon as I'm finished here."

"Leaving it? But aren't we going to be taking the boat back to your dock on Lake Jesup?"

"No, Princess. This barge isn't bad for hiding out on, but it's too slow for our purposes at this point. We need to get back to Pulse Points, pronto. If anyone here has any ideas about beating us there, I want to make sure they don't have a prayer of making it to the store before we do."

Eden folded her arms across her chest, shaking her head in confusion. "And exactly how do you propose to do that? We don't even have a car with us."

Completing the letter, Jack double-clicked on the mouse button and sent the e-mail message on its way. Stashing the diskette in the pocket of his shirt, along with the original ransom note, he leaned back in his chair as a cool, cocky grin spread slowly across his ruggedly handsome face. "No," he agreed smoothly, "we don't have a car, but we do have something even better. An alternative means of transportation." He rapped his knuckles against the hollow wall behind him, indicating some sort of well-concealed storage area. "A bike."

Eden glanced suspiciously at the wall where she could just make out the outline of an opening she hadn't noticed before. An oversized closet or doorway, she wasn't sure which. "A bike? You mean we're going to pedal our way back?"

"Not quite, Princess," he said, standing to unlatch the opening. The door swung downward, bird-wing style. "We're not going to pedal, but we are going to ride."

Eden swallowed hard at the awesome piece of machinery that could now be seen through the open doorway. "On that?" she asked. "A motorcycle?"

Actually, she decided, it was more like a chrome-armored monster of a motorcycle. Fierce, fire-breathing. Fast.

"Unless you can think of a better way to get back to Winter Park in a few hours flat."

Eden blinked in horror at the sleek, gleaming machine. "Don't you mean flattened?"

She didn't like motorcycles. Never had, never would. They were too big and loud, too overwhelming. Unfortunately, she couldn't think of a faster way back to the shop.

"What—what about your boat?" she asked, prolonging the inevitable.

"I'll leave it docked here, pick it up later."

"What about Babette?" she asked, in a last desperate, cowardly attempt to save herself.

"Pack her up snug in your purse and she'll be just fine. In fact, she'll probably love it."

"Oh, sure," she said, calling the poodle over and tucking her safely into the depths of her shoulder bag. "But if she pokes her head up for a look-see while we're riding, she's going to be one windblown biker puppy."

"You know, Ed," Jack said, laughing, "you just might love it yourself if you'd only let go a little."

Minutes later they were rolling down the road, and

as Jack took the bike up through the gears, Eden felt her adrenaline cranking right along with it.

She let out a deep breath and cracked one eye open, watching oak trees, Spanish moss, and palmettos fly past in a speeding blur. Love it? He was kidding, right? How could she let herself do that when the scenery itself was making her queasy?

Babette, on the other hand, didn't seem to mind the ride. The tip of her nose emerged from the top of Eden's handbag, followed shortly by the rest of her head. Her mouth lolled open in sheer canine pleasure as her tongue wagged and her tiny ears flew horizontally in the wind.

"She likes it!" Eden exclaimed, almost jealous of the poodle's obvious enjoyment.

Of Jack's too. He seemed to be totally exhilarated by the potent thrill of all that power rumbling forcefully beneath his fingertips. Hard muscles, horsepower, and pleasure. The combination was as heady as it was volatile.

Why couldn't she learn to let herself go like that, to fully feel the pleasure of the moment, just once? What would it be like to experience the excitement without the interference of fear? She envied his ability to do just that. To live only for the moment, for immediacy, to let the wind buffet him, no matter which way it blew.

It was several hours later when the bike finally roared to a stop just outside the shop. But only moments after that they were inside and on-line with the store's computer. With any luck some sort of answer might already be waiting for them.

"Anything from the kidnappers?" Jack asked.

"Hold on," she said, scrolling down through the unwanted mounds of junk mail and searching for the telltale name. "Here!" she exclaimed, highlighting the return address she'd been looking for. "There's one message. It's marked *'urgent.'* "

Her thumb was poised against the mouse button, preparing to double-click and call the kidnapper's answer up onto the screen, but something seemed to be stopping her. Whatever was contained in that message could have a dire effect on her future, not to mention Armand's. She wasn't sure she had the strength to read that message just at this moment.

She wasn't sure she even wanted to know what was in it.

NINE

Tears welled in Eden's eyes as her hand began to tremble over the keyboard. How could she be so selfish, worrying about her own future when Armand's very life hung in the balance?

"What's the problem, Princess?"

"I—I'm not sure. Just feeling a little shaky, I guess."

Shaky? She was feeling guilty. This entire ordeal might soon be over, and all at once she'd realized something really awful about herself. She wasn't feeling enough. The thought of having Armand safely returned to her didn't make her want to jump with joy. It left her numb, drained. Either she was totally stressed out from the events of the last few days, or she didn't deserve such a fine man.

"Would—would you mind reading the message for me?"

"Have a seat. Take a deep breath," he said, settling her comfortably into a tall chair behind the counter and gently stroking her under the chin as if she were a puppy in need of comfort.

"It's going to be fine," he reassured her. "Whatever the message, we'll handle it together."

She nodded, waiting patiently while he turned back to the computer screen and quickly called the e-mail up.

"Good news," he said quietly. "They've agreed to our terms."

Eden exhaled slowly. "They'll settle for the vial of scent, then, instead of the formula?"

"It looks that way. They want us to make the drop-off here, in the alley behind the shop."

"And if we do?"

"According to this, they'll set Herman free as soon as they're holding the goods."

She jumped to her feet, suddenly restless, and began to pace back and forth across the floor. "When?"

"First thing tomorrow," Jack told her. "At day-break."

She stopped dead in her tracks, turning to look at him. "Tomorrow! Oh. That soon?"

"You got it, Ed. Of course, there are no guaran-tees. . . ."

"Yes, but—tomorrow."

He folded his arms across his chest, looking down at her with those intense, all-seeing green eyes of his. "If I didn't know better, Princess, I'd say you were . . . am-biguous about all this."

"No!" she exclaimed. "Of course not. I'm simply relieved."

"I see. You sure that's all it is?"

"Certainly. Definitely. Naturally."

"Going to invite me to the wedding, Princess?"

"Invite you— Look, do you mind if we change the subject?"

She turned to the computer screen, searching for

something, anything that would distract her from a subject she found very, well, distracting. "Shouldn't we save this document, just in case?"

"Sounds like a good idea," he agreed, pulling the diskette from his shirt pocket and handing it to her.

Eden inserted it into the drive slot, selected the save icon and copied the page to disk. Exiting the program, she attempted to close the file, but apparently opened another one by mistake. A full-color picture popped up onto the screen. A picture of a little girl about seven or eight years old.

Jack swore softly behind her.

"Oh," Eden whispered, instantly realizing who the small, mischievous-looking child had to be. Lara. "That's her, isn't it?"

"*Was* her," he said, his voice tight, with no trace of emotion. "Guess you found my personal file on her, huh?"

"I didn't mean to. The disk wasn't marked."

"I never label my files," he explained, "until the case is ready to be closed. Fifteen years of searching," he said harshly, "and this is the only one still open."

Eden shook her head slowly, studying the petite, pixielike face in front of her. She'd been touched by Jack's story of his missing sister and how he'd spent so much of his life hunting for some trace of her. But it had never hit her as hard as it did now. Putting a face with the name only made the tragedy that much more real for her. And if the sight of the smiling child affected her so strongly, she could only imagine what it was doing to Jack.

Eating him up inside, most likely. And no wonder. The child was adorable, so full of life and fun, it was hard to face the possibility that she might not be alive any longer. No, it was impossible to face. Unthinkable. Which was exactly the way Jack had managed to deal with a loss so large.

He hadn't dealt with it at all.

"She's marvelous," Eden told him honestly. "Delightful. I can see the family resemblance. In the eyes, mostly. Not just the color but the spirit. I'll bet she is—was—pretty feisty."

"Feisty?" His voice behind her sounded surprised, almost annoyed.

Eden turned to look at him. "I meant it as a compliment. She doesn't look capable of sitting still for a second. Kind of like you."

"Is that how you see me, Ed?"

"Well, yes. Restless. Ready to move on at the drop of a hat."

"Incapable of settling down?"

"Aren't you?"

"It started out that way," he admitted. "It's gotten to be something of a habit by now."

Eden turned away, forcing her attention back to the screen. Jack wasn't the only one having a problem with facing reality. She didn't want to face the facts entirely herself. The fact that Jack Rafferty might be the sort of man she wanted, the man she was drawn to on some deep, sensual level, but he could never, ever be the sort of man she needed.

"Scroll down," Jack suggested, "and you can get a better idea of how she might look now."

"Now?" Eden repeated, confused. "She'd be, what, about twenty-three?" She pressed the page-down key until a second picture appeared on the screen, replacing the first. A picture of a softly smiling young woman who barely even resembled the original photo of the child.

"Are you saying that's her? I don't understand. Where did you get this picture?"

"That disk contains a specialized search program," he explained. "A tool that cops and investigators use to project what someone might look like under different circumstances. In this case I entered the required parameters from fifteen years ago and asked the program to come up with a visual of how Lara would appear today."

Eden studied the picture, trying to see the likeness between the little girl and the woman who stared vacuously out at her from the screen. There was very little as far as she could make out. The shape of the eyes was similar, the nose slightly firmer, the mouth more grown-up, but beyond that, she simply couldn't see it.

"So this is the image you've been using to search for her?" Eden asked.

He nodded briefly. "There's a long list of addresses on that disk too. Organizations, businesses, even individuals who are willing to publicly post the missing-person fliers and reward posters I send them. I've had some luck finding other folks that way, but very few leads for her."

"Jack," she said, shaking her head, "I've heard of these techniques before, and I guess they must work, but . . ."

"But?" he prompted.

"I'm sorry, but that picture really doesn't look at all the way I'd imagine Lara now."

There was momentary silence behind her, then a slow, smooth, scratching sound. Eden smiled to herself. She didn't have to turn around to picture exactly what Jack was doing. He was rubbing his hand against that stubborn, hard chin of his, ruminating thoughtfully about what she'd just said.

He took the stool she'd been sitting on earlier, pulled it up beside her. "Show me," he said.

"Is there some way to put both of these pictures together, side by side on the same screen?"

Wordlessly he punched in the computer commands, shrinking the size of both Lara renderings, dragging the older photo down the page until it was neatly aligned with the first.

"Good," she said, studying the screen. "Now take a really good look. Don't you see what I'm saying?"

He did look then, maybe closer than he had in many years. But the pictures appeared the same as they always had. The first was a snapshot of a beautiful little girl, taken at a happy moment in her young life. The second was a computer-enhanced image of a beautiful young woman.

He raked a hand through his hair, groaning inwardly. God, but it still hurt just to look at her. He didn't want to look. Didn't want to see.

"This is useless," he insisted, shutting his eyes in a futile effort to shut out the pain. But the face was still there, floating before him. The face that had haunted his dreams for as long as he could remember. "Hell, Ed," he swore fiercely, forcing himself to look again. "I've been through all this more than a thousand times. A million times. Nothing's changed."

"Maybe that's the problem," she said. "Maybe it's your image that needs updating instead of Lara's."

"Huh?"

"Don't you think it's just the least bit odd that we're both looking at the exact same photos but seeing entirely different things? On the left I see a little girl who was playful, impish. A sweet-faced scamp with leaves in her hair, a smudge on her cheek, and a twinkle in her eye. What do you see?"

With an effort he studied the picture again. A scamp? An imp? The Lara he remembered hadn't been either of those things. She'd been sweet, well behaved, neat and tidy. Near perfect. Blinking at the picture now, he realized that recollection might not be entirely realistic.

"What are you saying, Ed? That I've idealized the memory of her?"

"Maybe just a little," she told him gently.

Was it possible? Was the picture he'd been carrying around in his head at odds with the image on the screen before him? Come to think of it, he'd been the one to take that snapshot.

The scene of that day flashed back through his mind. She'd been tumbling in a pile of leaves, wrestling with Wolf. She'd refused to come when he called, sticking her tongue out at him defiantly. He'd rewarded her rascally behavior with a smart tap to her dirt-encrusted, blue-jeaned behind.

"So maybe she was a pistol," he admitted. "A troublemaking little monkey as a matter of fact. So what?"

"So, this young woman on the right looks as neat as a nun and twice as nice. More like a Stepford sister than a real one."

Jack shook his head slowly, still trying to come to grips with the truth. His gut told him that Ed was right, that he had been filtering out every not-so-perfect memory of his rapscallion of a little sister and replacing the facts with fiction. The result was an image every bit as unrealistic as Ed's projection of her ideal man.

Herman was not all she made him out to be in her

mind. He'd been trying to show her that for days. Instead she was showing him.

Perspective. Apparently he'd lost his completely on the same day he'd lost Lara. No, his little sister hadn't even been close to perfect. Still, he'd loved her anyway.

Love. To Jack's way of thinking, it was a four-letter word. So was *hope*, come to think of it. They were cruel, relentless emotions, both of them. They'd betrayed him before. Blinded him for fifteen years.

And now Ed was asking him what? To place his faith in them again? To open himself up for more agony? That was exactly what would happen if he revised the vision of Lara in his brain, along with the version on the screen.

"Leave it alone, Princess," he said.

"No, Tracker Jack. You saved me once, now it's my time to try and save you. Assuming you're *worth* saving, which is still debatable at this point."

"Exactly what are you proposing, Princess?"

"Fix the photo. Print up a new batch of fliers and posters on the shop printer, here, and send them out."

"Now?"

"We're going to be waiting around here until daybreak anyway, aren't we? And unless you can think of something better to do . . ."

As a matter of fact, he could. Several fascinating possibilities immediately crossed his mind. Graphic, gut-wrenching images that involved Ed flat on her back beneath him, asking him for something she had never known before. Her first glimpse of paradise. He wanted to be the one to take her there.

"No," she said, "don't answer that! Let's get straight to work instead. We'll start with the hair. Heavens, where did you come up with that do, anyway?"

"Hey, I thought it was nice. Ladylike."

"Little-old-lady-like is more like it. She's supposed to be twenty-three, not a hundred and three."

Grumbling loudly, he grabbed for the keyboard, manipulated the cut and paint program keys, and ruthlessly chopped off Lara's long, prim locks, opting for a shorter, sportier style.

"Better already," she told him. "Now for the mouth."

"What's the matter with it?"

"Nothing, if she's currently employed as an IRS auditor. It's firm. Too stern. She ought to be smiling. No, grinning, the way you do sometimes. Yes, give her the Rafferty grin."

Having no clear idea exactly what sort of expression that was, he changed the straight line of her mouth from serious at the corners to curving and halfway upturned.

"Excellent!" she exclaimed. "Now we're getting somewhere. She looks more like herself. Almost jaunty."

Jaunty? He didn't know about that, but she did look a lot closer to the adult version of the slightly troublesome tomboy he now remembered. Much better than the neat, dressed-up doll he'd made her out to be before.

"Okay. Now, ditch the dress. That adorable little neck bow," she insisted, "has got to go."

"I don't know, Princess," he said, reluctant to give up that last, cherished image. "I've always thought it was pretty sweet."

"It is," she agreed. "So sweet I'm convinced Lara is way too cool to wear it today. No sister of yours would have the poor fashion sense to put on such a thing."

"All right, all right. The bow is history." Mercilessly

he deleted it from the photo, adding a simple white button-down collar in its place. The result was far less fancy and feminine, but less distracting as well. Now the major focus was directed on Lara's face. "Anything else?"

"Nope," she said. "Now she really does look right."

Jack folded his arms across his chest, studying the final portrait they'd come up with. The changes were dramatic, but he had to admit, they were probably much more realistic than his original, china-doll version. He'd been deluding himself for so long, it had taken a fresh pair of eyes to point out the obvious. Lara didn't belong on the pedestal he'd made for her in his mind. She deserved to be remembered as the down-to-earth, high-spirited person she'd always been.

"Well?" Eden asked him.

"Well, Princess, let's print up a hundred or so and see what happens."

An hour later they were seated at a worktable in the back room, stuffing envelopes. Here in the sheltered, high-ceilinged space, it was quiet, lit by the glow of a dusty, cut-crystal chandelier. But outside, night had fallen. Probably the last night he and Ed would be spending together, Jack realized.

This wasn't exactly the way he'd imagined passing the time with her. Not that he wasn't grateful for her help. The thing she'd done for him, was doing for him now, was one of the most selfless acts he could imagine. Her own future hung in the balance tonight. Whatever happened in the morning would likely decide that future one way or another. But instead of worrying about her own problems, she was supporting him with his.

No woman had ever done anything like it for him before.

Up until now he'd been in the habit of giving help. The concept of getting help was still completely foreign. Hell, he hadn't been willing to accept it from Ed until she'd put her foot down and told him the way it was going to be.

The woman was a pistol, hot as a firecracker with a very long fuse and every bit as dangerous. She could strut around in her uptown suits, wear silk designer stockings, and put her hair up like a continental French sophisticate, but no amount of cosmopolitan gloss could hide the true essence inside her.

She was still a sensual temptress at heart. A woman who felt more than most, experienced sensations more than most. Every sensation, that is, but one. She'd never experienced a sexual climax. And if Herman was returned to her first thing tomorrow, it was pretty certain that she never would.

For a lady like Ed to miss out on such a joyous part of life didn't bear thinking about. She was made to make love to a man, made to let a man love her back. Every heightened sense she'd been born with was perfectly tuned in to the slightest nuances of physicality. To focus in on her feelings as well as the person she was experiencing them with.

Jack wanted to be that person. He wanted to help her experience the sensations he knew she was capable of. Hell, he wanted to feel them himself.

"That's the last of them," she said, sealing the final envelope and adding it to the neatly stacked pile on top of the long wooden worktable. "The only thing left to do is mail them out. We can do that first thing tomorrow."

"First thing tomorrow we'll be making the ransom drop, Ed."

"Oh, right."

"If everything goes well, you'll be back in Herman's arms by then. Stuffing a mailbox with fliers is going to be the last thing on your mind."

"Of course."

"I appreciate your help, though."

"I—it was the least I could do after what you've done for me."

"I'd like to do more, Princess. If you'd only let me."

The silence stretched between them as Eden considered exactly what he'd just said to her. Was he suggesting . . ? Nervously wetting her lips, she glanced at him, trying to make out his meaning. His gaze was intense, as piercing and penetrating as deep emerald crystals. Yes, she realized, he was suggesting that. She understood what he meant with every fiber of her being.

He was offering to make love to her.

Flustered, her face flushing wildly, she stood up from her chair, restacking the neat piles of envelopes which were already perfectly aligned. "I'm sure you've done enough already," she said politely, pretending not to understand.

"Ed," he said, looking up at her with an expression hot and hypnotic enough to seduce nuns. "I haven't even gotten started."

If that was true, Eden thought wildly, just what did he call the encounter they'd had back at the bungalow? *Foreplay.* He'd already raised the level of that to an art form. She could only imagine what would happen if she let him have free rein with her. Judging by the look in his eyes, there was no doubt that *he* was imagining it at the moment.

Vividly.

"I'm sure I don't know what you're talking about,"

she insisted, feeling as frantic under that sexual stare of his as a deer caught helplessly in headlights.

He stood, kicked his chair back, and began to approach her slowly from the opposite side of the table. "I'm sure you do."

Swallowing hard, Eden tried to stand her ground, but she knew what would happen if she let him get too close to her. Heaven help her, she *knew*. "That perfume must be around here somewhere," she began to babble, edging her way toward the scent organ as Jack edged his way toward her. "It's probably a good idea if I find it now, right away, just so we'll be prepared for the morning. Don't you agree? Now, where did I put it?"

"Ed," he soothed, "it's no use. I'm not going to let you change the subject this time. We need to talk about it."

Something deep and shivery way down in her belly told her that talking wasn't what Jack had on his mind. *She* certainly wasn't thinking about it. She was too busy remembering the way he'd looked back at the bungalow, bare chested, hard bodied, sexier than sin. She was remembering the things he'd done to her with that body, with that mouth, those hands. The hands of an artist, a sensual sculptor who knew how to mold her, stroke her, to shape her being so beautifully, she barely even recognized her own responses.

"Here it is!" she exclaimed a little wildly as she reached into a hidden corner of the desk and latched onto the small vial of scent. "I'd almost forgotten where I'd left it." With shaking hands she anxiously uncorked the bottle and tested the scent with a quick whiff. "Yes, that's it all right. Did I tell you it was a present from Herman? I mean Armand!"

"Princess," he said, closing in on her, "what is it you're so afraid of?"

"Nothing," she said, a little desperate. "You want to talk about it? Okay, let's talk. I appreciate the offer, really, but I don't need it. I'm not some sexual charity case!"

"No," he agreed, "you're a nut case."

"Thank you so much."

"I mean it, Ed. You've got to be crazy if you think I want to make love to you out of pity."

"Why, then?"

He came forward, held out his hands, closed them over hers. "Because of this," he said, dropping a light kiss on the top of her head, "and this," he said, moving his mouth to her forehead and brushing his lips against her, "and this," he said, stroking her cheek with his own. "Because I've barely even touched you, Princess, and you're already *ready* for me, aren't you?"

"No," she lied, her hands shaking so badly that several drops of the perfume spilled out from the open vial she'd been clinging to. The precious scent rolled down between her tightly clenched palms, trickling to the tips of her fingers and ultimately dripping onto his.

Horrified, she pulled her hands away, glancing down at the half-empty bottle, feeling as if it weren't simply perfume she'd just spilled, but blood. Armand's blood. If there was nothing left to deliver to the kidnappers in the morning, he was as good as dead. Thank goodness there was some scent remaining at the bottom of the glass, but no thanks to her.

Carefully she clamped her fingers over the top of the bottle and recorked it. What had come over her? She was holding her fiancé's life in her hands and she still couldn't stop herself from thinking about another man.

Wanting another man. She did want Jack to make love to her, she realized. Badly.

So badly that she was actually considering risking everything she thought she'd ever wanted for just one night with him.

"Put the bottle down."

She didn't move. She couldn't.

"Put it down," he repeated. "I don't want to be responsible for what happens to it."

Eden set the vial safely back in the corner.

"Good. I have no intention of turning Herman into some sort of martyr in your mind." He folded his arms across his chest, leaned back against the worktable, and watched her with a directness that was nearly as unnerving as his touch had been. "I'd prefer to banish him from your head completely."

Eden's chin went up. There was something about that supremely confident, almost cocky attitude of his that made her want to challenge him. Who did he think he was, anyway? God's gift to women? Heaven's prize sent just for her?

Apparently he was so secure in his sexual prowess that he had no doubt of his ability to satisfy her. He was certain, in fact, that he could take her to a place her future husband could not. To go, so to speak, where no man had gone before.

Lord help her, but she hoped he was right.

She folded her arms across her chest, matching him body language for body language. "How do you propose to do that?"

"Come here and I'll be more than happy to show you."

The wind went out of her sails at that. A verbal

challenge was one thing. Putting herself within easy reach was another matter entirely.

"No, thanks," she said, prepared for further arguments.

Unfortunately, he didn't argue any further. He simply shrugged his broad shoulders at her and accepted her answer. "Fine," he said. "Suit yourself."

"Fine?" she repeated, strangely disappointed in his entirely unexpected response. He'd been promising to take her to paradise and he was willing to stop at a single "No, thanks"?

His smile was lazy, amused. "What were you expecting, Princess?"

"I—I don't know."

"I can't choose for you, Ed," he said. "You have to make the decision yourself."

The decision. She'd been trying to avoid it for days now, trying to deny what she felt for him, what she wanted to feel *with* him, if only for a short, sweet time. For one night. Instinctively she knew that a single evening, no matter how ecstatic, would be all that Jack was able to give her.

He was a loner by habit, as well as by nature. She knew that he cared for her in his own restless way, but emotionally he remained unavailable. The disappearance of his sister had left him deprived in that department. Under circumstances like that, how could she blame him for holding back? There was still so much pain in his heart over the loss he'd suffered, there simply wasn't room for another woman.

It was ironic, really, that the one thing she'd looked for most of her life was the single thing Jack couldn't deliver to her. Security, stability. Long-term commitment.

All of the qualities her father had lacked. Sooner or later, no matter how strong the passion between them promised to be, he was bound to do exactly the same thing her dad had done. He was destined to leave her.

Even more ironic was the realization that the man she was engaged to could never fulfill the need she felt now for total, physical release. The need she'd only become aware of since the first day she'd laid eyes on Jack Rafferty.

"So, I really have to decide?"

"Ms. Wellbourne, you don't have to do anything."

"And if I said that I wanted to—to—you know. What if I did say that I want to try?"

"They don't call us *private* investigators for nothing," he said jokingly.

"That's not funny."

"Oh, no? Then why are you smiling?"

"Terror? Anticipation? Lord, I have no idea what I'm feeling anymore. I only know I'm not supposed to be feeling anything around you."

"Maybe you're being too hard on yourself, Ed. You're not letting yourself feel anything at all."

Was he right? she wondered. Was she being too hard on herself, expecting something she would never dream of asking from someone else? Facing the rest of her life as a married woman with no prospect of ever experiencing physical fulfillment was a lot to ask of anyone. But she wasn't married. Yet.

The option was still open to her. After the wedding vows it wouldn't be. But the decision she had to make went far beyond the physical. The connection she felt with Jack was deeper than that, stronger. It was empathetic, emotional.

She wanted to join with him on some level that

would help to heal them both. This wasn't just about what he could do for her, it was what they might be able to do for each other. Even if the moment was fleeting, it was one she didn't want to let go of. She wanted to catch it, hold it, make it last for the rest of her life if she had to.

She did want him to make love to her. But even more certainly, she wanted to make love to him back. He would never, ever admit it, she realized, but Jack needed this night as much as she did herself. Drawing in a deep breath, she silently promised them both that they would never forget it.

Okay," she said, "I've decided."

TEN

"I want to," Ed told him.

I want to. Jack decided they were possibly the three sweetest words ever spoken in the entire English language. His Princess had just given him the most incredible gift he could imagine. Her trust.

The simple idea of it made his gut squeeze tight with powerfully protective instincts. His first impulse was to gather her up in his arms and hug her until she could barely breathe. His second was to lay her flat out on her back on the table and fulfill every imaginable need. Her needs, he thought wryly, not his.

So much for keeping his emotions under careful control. So much for not becoming personally involved. The very nature of his thoughts revealed he was already in way over his head. *He was drowning*. He'd been fantasizing about making love to this woman for days, and now that the moment had finally arrived, the only thing he could think of was pleasing *her*.

He hoped he could prove himself worthy of her. For the first time in his life he hoped he could *prove* himself.

Never had he wanted to satisfy a woman so badly before.

That's what he wanted for Ed. But was she really ready to handle it?

"Princess," he said, "you have to be sure about this. Damn sure."

The words were out before Jack had a chance to completely consider them. What was he saying? What he thinking? The sexiest, finest, most desirable woman he'd ever known was all but offering herself to him and he was arguing with her about it? Lord, but he had to be crazy. Either that or . . .

He had it so bad for Ed he couldn't see straight. Much worse than he'd realized before.

She came toward him, her amber eyes wide and wanting, needy with feelings she was too innocent to name. Innocent, that's what Ed was, in spite of her outward sophistication, in spite of the fact that she'd been with a man before. In spirit his Princess was still a virgin, unaware of the ultimate intimacy two lovers could share. The idea that he could still be her first was mindblowing enough. The realization that he was reconsidering his actions for her sake shook him straight to his core.

"I'm *positive*," she said, stopping a few feet in front of him, just out of arm's reach. "I'm ready. What do you want me to do?"

Jack swallowed hard as muscles fisted deep inside him. What did he want her to do? God, but she couldn't be that innocent, she couldn't be totally unaware of what an offer like that might do to a man. Desire clutched his groin, sudden and sharp. He wanted her to leave, now, to turn tail and run before he had a chance to lay his undeserving paws on her. He wanted to save her from himself.

"Princess," he said, "you don't know what you're doing. We need to rethink this whole thing before it goes any further."

Was it really his own voice that had just said those incredibly idiotic words? Impossible. What sort of altruistic insanity had just come over him? *Bad*, he thought silently. Lord, but he really had it bad.

The disappointment on her face unnerved him even more than her initial offer had. "Why?" she whispered. "Don't you want me?"

With every bone in his body, Jack thought. Like he'd never wanted any other woman in his life.

"That's beside the point," he said hoarsely.

Her eyes were huge, her pupils dilated to twin pools of flame-warmed whiskey. "But I thought—aren't you—aroused by me?"

He was rigid as a jackhammer. So hard it hurt. And he hadn't even touched her.

"Because," she went on, "I think I can do something about that. I mean, I may be frigid, but I can still . . . participate."

The thing she did next made the air rush straight from his lungs. Reaching for the front of her own blouse, she began to strip, slowly popping the buttonholes open, one by one. The garment spread wide, slipped from her shoulders, dropped to the floor. Jack's jaw nearly dropped right along with it.

"Ed," he groaned, "what the hell do you think you're doing?"

"Picking up where Snake Woman left off," she informed him, kicking her shoes from her feet. "I'm a quick learner."

His gaze narrowed dangerously. "Cut it out, Princess. This isn't some game we're playing here."

"No," she agreed, "it isn't a game. It's a show. And you're going to watch every second of it."

She turned her attention to her shorts, slowly unzipping them, letting the cotton fabric join the shirt at her feet.

Jack swore softly. She was making it all but impossible for him to walk away. She was making it hard. Damn *hard*. A man had his limits, after all. Altruism could only last so long in the face of a sight like that. A Princess in a French lace bra and soft silk panties. The temptation was almost too much. Almost.

"Stop it," he said sternly. "Or pretty soon you're not going to be able to stop me."

"Isn't that the idea?" she said, reaching around for the hook that was holding together the back of her bra.

Her idea, he thought fiercely, not his. Exactly who was seducing who here?

How much longer was he going to hold out? Why was he even trying to? The answer was right in front of him, in the limpid look of her eyes, the beautiful, sexual flush of her skin. She'd been denying her physical needs for so long, she was aching for what he could give her, making him ache for it as well.

Jack wanted to soothe that ache inside her; he wanted to be the man who would finally set her essence free. The problem was, he wasn't sure how to do it without hurting her. Shattering the walls she'd erected around herself might also mean shattering her dream.

She wasn't in love with Herman, that much he knew. But she was in love with the idea of him. Long-term commitment. "I do until I die." Those were her particular fantasies, the ones she'd cherished since childhood.

They were ideals she felt so strongly about, she was prepared to spend the rest of her life with a man who was totally wrong for her.

Who was he to take those dreams away from her? The right man? Yeah. In *his* dreams.

He couldn't give her the life she wanted. How could he when he didn't even have a life of his own? It hadn't been his since the day Lara had disappeared. Asking Ed to share it with him would require an enormous sacrifice on her part, a sacrifice no woman should have to make.

The fact that he was even considering the possibility proved just how much he cared for her already. Too much for a man who had nothing to offer her. Nothing, that is, except one night of ecstasy.

No, he couldn't give Ed her happily-ever-after.

But he could give her this night.

Dammit, he would give her this night. And he would make the passion last as long as possible, till morning if his body could manage it, because the memory of it would have to last the rest of their lives.

Urgently, almost angrily, he grabbed her by the arm, stopping her torturous striptease. "No," he said, backing her up against the table until there was no place left for her to move. "This isn't going any further. At least, it isn't going any further without my help."

Eden's heart leapt to her throat at the sudden urgency of Jack's reaction. Finally! She'd been trying to incite him, behaving so brazenly, she barely recognized herself. But she needed him so badly, she'd felt powerless to stop. If stripping in front of him was what it took, she'd been bound and determined to follow through with it.

Now it seemed that he was bound and determined to finish what she'd started. He'd practically nailed her backside to the table with his full-court press toward her, but his efforts didn't stop there. He wrapped his hands around her waist, lifted her bodily onto the work-table, letting her legs drape down, mingling with his. One hand came up, his fingers tracing slowly, toying and teasing, along the lacy fabric covering that stretched across the top of her bra.

Eden closed her eyes, sighing.

"Oh, no, Princess," he said, lifting her chin with his free hand. "No fair. I want you to look at me. I want you to see *everything* I'm doing. And I want to watch the way those eyes of yours light up in response."

Eden's gaze flew open. Goodness, but he wasn't go-ing to let her avoid a single second of the experience. He intended her to see it all, feel it all, everything she could handle. Maybe even more.

Instinctively, Eden arched toward him, the memory of the pleasure he'd given her before still fresh in her mind. She wanted to feel his hands on her again, every-where.

Only he didn't touch her. He dragged the lace of her bra downward, instead, baring her breats, fully exposing them to his view. Her nipples budded from the scratch of the fabric, peaking with pleasure as Jack's stare took in the half-naked length of her. Eden's heart went a little crazy as he studied her, his gaze darkening at the physical evidence of her growing desire.

"Lord, yes," he said, "you are beautiful." He caught her up in his arms, pulling her close.

Her breasts brushed against the firmness of his chest. His arousal nudged her thighs. Eden gasped softly. He was hard already. The thought of what he was going to do to her with all that amazing male equipment sent a thrill of excitement spearing through her.

But apparently he wasn't going to do anything with it just yet. Not until he'd thoroughly tortured her with the sweet agony of anticipation. He pulled back again, still fascinated with the way her breasts rode high against the dark lace. Eden's breath caught, waiting for him to explore that part of her with his hands as well as his eyes. Her stomach muscles knotted, her back arched slightly, inviting him to sample her there.

Still, he didn't. He dropped to his knees in front of her instead, gently spreading her thighs apart with his hands. His blond hair tickled the inside of her legs. Eden's face flushed hotly.

"Oh, no," she whispered, softly shocked. "Please, not that."

"Oh, yes," Jack whispered back, slowly dragging her panties down, "that."

Every muscle in Eden's body squeezed and tightened with apprehension, with embarrassment, but also with need. The idea of him putting his mouth on her *there* was terrifying and intensely exciting all at once. Lord, she couldn't let him do that to her. The feelings would surely kill her. But then again, what a way to die.

Seconds later she was completely naked from the waist down. Cool air whispered between her legs, and then the caressing warmth of Jack's breath. Eden's hands went over her eyes and she moaned softly.

"Don't hide your feelings," Jack told her. "Don't hide your face. Look at what I'm doing to you, Princess. Watch every minute of what happens. I never want you to forget."

Just when she was about to reassure him that amnesia was impossible at such a moment, his lips touched the tender flesh that lined the insides of her thighs. Her hands came down and clutched the edge of the table.

Her eyes flew open, not missing a second. Her heart was hammering so wildly, she wondered if she would pass out before he even touched her there. There in the spot that throbbed for him the most.

His tongue rimmed the very highest edges of her thighs, concentrating first on one side, then the other, kissing, licking, sweetly exploring the very edges of her being. Eden's chest squeezed and tightened with apprehension, with need. Her knuckles were white against the table, but she still held on, preparing for the sensations that she knew were coming next. *Praying* for the sensations that would assuage the incredible ache he'd started inside her.

He worked his way slowly, exquisitely toward her mound. She swayed beneath the tender, terribly erotic sensations he was causing. Her legs were trembling faintly, shaking as she waited for his touch, wanting it, yet fearing what the feel of him there would do to her. Every nerve in her body was aroused and ready, every fiber yearned with white-hot need. Her hands clutched his head, her fingers wound through his soft, golden hair.

Moments ago she thought she'd die if he kissed her there. Now she knew she was going to die if he didn't.

"Jack," she said, "please . . ."

His hands tightened around her thighs, anchoring her to the table. "Hang on, Princess," he whispered against her. "Hang on to me."

Then finally, fully, he covered her very core with his mouth and tasted her.

"Oh, *God*," she moaned.

His kiss deepened, exploring her depths, suckling and drinking her in. Eden breathed in sharply as the sensations surged through her, wild and sweet, seizing and clutching at her body. If Jack hadn't been holding her, restraining her, she would surely have slipped to the floor.

He continued to taste her there, continued exploring her with his tongue as if he were a starving man and she was the single source of nourishment he could not live without. Eden was certain she *was* dying then, dying and going straight up to heaven. Fire licked her veins, swirled through her blood. Her body grew more restless by the minute. Instead of assuaging her need, Jack was making it stronger.

She was hovering near some high, ecstatic peak, hovering but not quite reaching it.

A frustrated whimper escaped her.

Jack pulled back, stood to soothe her. "Easy, Princess," he said, stroking her hair, "we're getting there."

She moaned again, sensually, straining and nuzzling against him with pent-up desire. She was so responsive, he thought. So wildly sexy, he could've easily brought her to a climax several minutes ago. Too easily. She'd waited so long for this pleasure, he wanted to make it last. As long as he could humanly handle it.

At the moment he didn't know how long that would be. Those sweet little whimpers of hers were arousing him like crazy. Every soft, achy moan, every agonized gasp sent potent shafts of energy slamming straight to his groin. The sight of her, too, made his gut ache with fire. Her large, liquid eyes, half wild with need. Her beautifully bare breasts, overflowing from the top of her bra. Her dusky nipples, tautened and trembling, outlined with lace.

He couldn't stop himself from putting his hands on them. He wanted to feel how hard they were for himself, how hard the sight of them was making him at this second. He pulled and stroked at the peaking tips, taking the tightly drawn centers between his fingertips and rotating gently. Ed writhed against him, letting out sweet, shuddering cries. The sound brought him soaring pleasure.

He wrapped his arms around her back, released her bra and let her breasts flow free. He touched them again, fondling and caressing, feeling their enticing weight in his palms. But it wasn't enough to satisfy him. Or her.

He bent to take them into his mouth, tasting and lathing each one in turn. Ed's moans came faster, inciting him to the point of pain. She was that wrought up, that excitable. So much so that he could sense her react to a single flick of his tongue, hear her gasp as his suckling grew stronger, feel her thighs clutching against his as her need for him began to reach a fever pitch. He might be making her crazy with wanting, but slowly and surely the woman was driving him wild.

Still, he didn't stop. He couldn't have stopped at that moment, even if he'd wanted to, so great was his insatiable hunger. Somehow he couldn't get enough of her. He took more of her in, raining wet kisses across the sweetness of her flesh, gradually eating her up.

"Jack," she begged, her breath warm and ragged, *"please.* Please make love to me now."

He drew back, smiling, dropped a kiss on her nose. "What do you think I'm doing, Princess?"

"Torturing me," she whispered in frustration. "You're making me crazy for you, hot for you. You're making me—"

"What, Princess?" he asked, slipping his hand below her waist. "What, baby? Let me hear you say it."

"*Wet* for you," she admitted, nearly choking on the word.

"Am I?" he asked softly, checking it out for himself. His fingers delved inside her, feeling delicate muscles tighten and clench beneath his touch. Moist, slick muscles that responded as softly as rain-drenched flower petals to every probing, plundering move he made.

Ed cried out in sharp pleasure as her head arched backward. Her breast rose, presenting itself beautifully before him. He took the nipple between his teeth, tugging gently as his hand continued to explore and stroke her wetness down below. A low groan escaped him as his muscles contracted in excruciating response to hers.

"That's it, baby," he said. "Feel it. All of it."

Ed gasped, feeling more than she'd ever thought herself capable of handling, and yet still wanting to feel more of him. All of him, deep inside her. "It's not *fair*," she groaned, instinctively grabbing for the back of his blue jeans, holding on for dear life. "You're still dressed."

He drew back again to look at her. A lazy grin crossed his face. "If I wasn't," he told her, "this would be over by now."

"Oh," Eden whispered, a little awed by how much he seemed to want her. His gaze was hungry, mesmerized, erotically energized with deep male arousal. He wasn't the only one with the power, she realized. He might be playing her body beautifully, drawing responses from it that would make a concert pianist jealous, but she was affecting him too.

Her hands worked their way to the front of his jeans, testing her theory. His whole body shuddered in response when she touched him there. Yes, he was nearly as agonized with passion as she was. Impetuously she put her hand on his zipper, slowly working it down.

A low, urgent moan sounded. His, hers? She wasn't sure which.

Her hand reached inside, closed over him, trembling.

His eyes closed, wincing with pleasure. Encouraged, Eden ran her fingers up and down the massive length of him, stroking him boldly. Jack's jaw clenched. He made a harsh male sound, urgent, aggressive.

From that point, everything escalated.

He started shedding clothes at an Olympic pace, first the boots, then the shirt, and finally the blue jeans and briefs. Eden didn't get a truly accurate idea of the havoc she'd wreaked until he stood before her, naked and awesomely aroused. Heavens, but he was enormously rigid.

As excited as she was, as achy and wet, the unadulterated sight of him scared her. She'd thought she wanted him to penetrate her as quickly as possible. But staring now at exactly what he planned to penetrate her with, she wasn't so sure anymore.

"Take it easy," he said, as if reading her thoughts, "we're going to take it slow."

Even if it killed him, Jack warned himself silently, which at this point it probably would. He was going to make it right for her, no matter what. He was going to make it right or die trying.

Ignoring his agony, he tipped her head back and made passionate love to her mouth. Her lips parted willingly at his tender probing, inviting him to explore her with his tongue. Forgetting her fear, she opened everything up for him again. Her mouth, her arms. Her legs. They all wrapped around him, hugging him close.

The gesture was so sweet, so totally trusting, Jack's heart turned over in his chest.

He stopped again to look at her, taking her chin in his hands, forcing her gaze to lock with his. "This is it, Princess," he warned her, "the point of no return. We can still stop right here if you want to."

They were the words of insanity, he realized. The words of a man who'd completely lost his head for a woman. He couldn't quite believe he was saying them.

If she took him up on the offer and asked him to stop, he'd likely be damaged for life. Still, he would stop if she wanted. He would do *anything* she wanted.

Luckily she wanted more.

A tear squeezed slowly from the corner of her eye, a perfect drop of essence from the wellspring within her. "Make love to me," she urged him, her hand fluttering over him again, guiding him tremulously toward her.

Willingly, Jack proceeded to oblige her, positioning himself at her soft, satin opening. Cupping her buttocks, he drew in a deep breath, and made a slow, searing thrust. Ed's eyes widened beautifully, her nostrils flaring with need.

"Yes," she said, moving against him. "More."

A woman after his own heart, Jack realized, then corrected the thought as suddenly as it had emerged. She was a woman who already had his heart.

The need within him that had been urgent before suddenly became imperative. He had to have her. Now. All of him inside the sweetness of her.

He thrust again, deeper this time, and felt her tightness enveloping more of him. The excitement within him was violent, wrenching, but he wasn't sure if she could take him all in this way. She was so tender and tight, he was afraid the position would hurt her if her thrust any further.

"More," she whispered, squeezing his waist with her long, long legs.

She was frantic for him, Jack realized, overwhelmed with urgency. Maybe even more enflamed than he was at the moment, if such a state were possible. Muscles worked hard in his jaw as he picked her up bodily, still holding her to him, and impaled himself deeper inside her.

Her nails raked her back, inciting him further, but something warned him to stop. Resistance. She was definitely too small to experience him this way.

She pleaded with him sweetly, kissing him everywhere she could reach, begging him wildly for release. He'd never known a woman so incensed with pleasure, so full of female sensuality.

"Not like this, Princess," he said, soothing her with his voice. "It's not going to work this way."

"Make it work." She moaned weakly, aroused almost to the point of agony. "Make it work, or I'm going to die."

"I will," he said, withdrawing himself with an effort that was close to superhuman and lowering her to stand in front of him.

Her frustrated cries cut through him sharply. She dropped her head to his chest, whimpering. "It hurts," she said. "I want you so badly it hurts."

The pain Jack felt in that one moment had nothing to do with physical frustration and everything to do with a flood of emotion. Suddenly he was racked with feelings he couldn't name, overwhelmed with something he had no experience at handling. A spear lanced his heart. He looked down at Ed, speechless, struck with empathetic awareness. He hurt for her. Yearned for her. Experienced her agony as if it were his own. He couldn't bear the thought that he'd brought it on her himself.

"Princess," he whispered hoarsely, "I'm sorry."

"No, no," she said softly, coming to life again in his arms, kissing his neck, his chest, working her way down to his waist. "Don't be sorry," she said. "I'm not. I just want you to know how I feel. Terrible. Wonderful. I want to make you feel it, too, all of it, just the way you showed me."

Before he had a chance to assure her that he *did* feel it, desperately, she dropped to her knees in front of him. Jack's heart dropped to his knees as well.

"Ed," he choked roughly, "*no.*"

Didn't she realize what that would do to him at this moment? Didn't she realize what kind of effort he was expending already to hold himself back for her sake? She was toying with danger, striking a match against a stick of dynamite that was only minutes away from exploding.

"Yes," she said wickedly. "If I can take it, so can you."

As she took him into her mouth his own mouth went dry. Every fiber of his being wanted to scream out, to swear violently at the searing, soaring agony she was bringing him. Pleasure and pain merged instantly together as he fought to maintain some semblance of control. Her tongue was exquisite torture, her lips hot as acid as they worked their way up and down his shaft. His eyes clamped shut as he struggled for sanity. A low growl sounded deep in his throat as he realized it really was too much for him to handle.

He pulled away from her fiercely, caught her up in

his arms, and carried her over to the chaise lounge. "Now you've done it," he said, laying her flat out on her back beneath him. "I warned you, Princess, but I'm going to have to finish what you started."

He loomed over her, out of control, a predator in the throes of some primitive need. No more Mr. Nice Guy, he thought. No more Mr. Slow and Sweet. He was wild, an animal in pain, a man about to perform an act of simple self-preservation. If he didn't take her now, right now, he would expire.

She blinked up at him, shuddering with arousal, almost as wild as he was.

Almost.

He groaned inwardly, realizing that this position, too, had its perils. If he had her this way, he wouldn't be able to last for long. Maybe not long enough to give her what she needed. Hell, in his condition he wouldn't be able to hold out for ten seconds.

"Hold on, Princess," he said, "I have a better idea."

"What?"

"Stand up," he said, pulling her to her feet, and settling himself back down on the chaise in front of her.

"Oh," she said, a little unsure. "Me? On top?"

"You," he groaned, pulling her toward him. "On top of me, Princess. It's the only way you're going to have any control."

Tentatively she straddled him, her legs on either side of his waist, her silken softness so near, he could barely breathe. "Like this?"

"Like that, baby," he assured her, holding her by the waist and easing himself toward her entrance.

Experimentally she rotated her hips on top of him, touching his tip to her opening. Jack's jaw clenched hard. His need for her was so strong, he was close to biting himself on the tongue just to keep from yelling out. Her body shuddered forward, and he took one of her breasts into his mouth, trying to satisfy himself by suckling on her.

It was Eden who cried out instead. Her breasts were so tender by now, so swollen and turgid with need, that Jack's touch lanced through her like lightning. His tongue flicked across her, teasing, tempting. He sipped and stroked until she could feel the pull of him all the way down to her belly.

Below her belly she felt the pull of another part of him. His hands pushed firmly, guiding her downward, but her movements were already instinctive. Rocking slowly, she eased the tip of him inside her, sighing and shivering at the sweet urgency she felt. The fear was gone now. The hesitation left her, along with any last remnants of shyness. She was a woman in such terrible, beautiful need that nothing else mattered but fulfilling it.

Nothing else mattered but him.

His scent was everywhere, all around her, clinging like a warm male caress to the sex-heated surface of her skin. She drank it in deeply, reveling in the smell of him, in the wild, sweet way he was making her feel. She raised herself up, sinking forcefully back down as she took nearly the full length of him into her.

"Yes, Princess," he said, calling her name. "Make it good for you," Jack told her, his voice sounding out to her from somewhere far away. "Make it right."

She felt him pulling her up again, plunging himself so fully inside her, he sank all the way up to the hilt.

The second he hit bottom, she was climaxing wildly.

She called out his name as the stars came out. The world shattered around her as wave after wave of ecstasy spilled out, washing over her. Her eyes blinked open, awed by the beauty of it. The wetness streamed down her cheeks, the waves turning suddenly to tears of joy.

Jack caught her up in his arms, hugging her close. "That's it, baby," he said, soothing her, "that's it. Now turn for me, Princess. Turn over and let me love you my way."

He'd held out so long, held himself back so fiercely that it would take nothing less than full frontal contact now for him to find his own release. He moved over her, plunging deeply, uncontrollably into her tender, pulsating flesh. He was astonished at her incredible responsiveness as she moved under him, meeting him movement for movement, thrust for thrust. Her muscles clutched at him, wildly abandoned, then shuddered again and released.

She was peaking again, Jack realized, in the throes of a second climax even stronger than the first. The thought of sharing that with her sent him over the edge. Ed's first shattering experience couldn't possibly have been any sweeter than his own. The feelings flooded out of him in a torrent of completion, of emotions so surging and tender, they nearly ripped his soul away.

He was naked before her in more ways than one. Physically. Emotionally. For the first time in his life the essence that flowed out of him was more than a simple male release. This time, with Ed, it was the miraculous elixir of love.

Love, he repeated in silent astonishment, staggered by the realization of how he really felt for this woman. Aw, hell, he thought desperately, gathering her up in his arms again as if he never wanted to let her go.

Love.

ELEVEN

The night passed for Eden in a blur of passion. Or more accurately, a dream of it. They made love for hours on end, reveling in the feel, the scent, the simple, pleasurable presence of each other. She didn't begin to feel completely fulfilled until she'd experienced her fourth climax of the evening, and still there was some part of her that just couldn't get enough of Jack.

It was almost as if she'd never really made love before in her life.

As dawn broke, she realized she hadn't. She'd had sex with another man all right, with Armand, to be specific. At the time, she'd thought that was what lovemaking was. She'd had nothing else to compare it to. She just hadn't known then how it could be between a man and a woman. How all-consuming and incredible. How physically and emotionally fulfilling.

Heaven help her, she knew now.

They were snuggled together on the chaise, wrapped in each other's arms. Eden rested her head on Jack's chest, so grateful for what he'd done for her. He'd shared one of life's greatest secrets with her, given her one of the most wonderful gifts imaginable—a stunning sample of the human experience.

But now that that choice was behind her, an even bigger one still loomed before her. She had to decide what to do next.

She had to choose who she was going to do it with.

Armand was secure, stable. A safety line to reality. A brilliant chemist far more interested in his work than in running around with other women. His family tree could be traced back through many generations of reliable, marrying men. The kind of men who stuck around to raise their children, passed their homes on to them as well as their businesses.

The kind of men who didn't leave.

That was the sort of family, the sort of life, Eden had imagined herself being a part of. Until she'd met Jack Rafferty.

Tracker Jack.

He was everything she'd never wanted in a man. Everything she'd never wanted and so much more.

A drifter. A loner. A man with no roots and no apparent desire to grow them anytime soon. A man so determined to chase down a memory that he could barely stick around long enough to make new ones. Barely.

Glancing up at him now, into that hard, handsome face, Eden knew the memory he'd made for her this night would never leave. No, the remembrance might not, but he surely would.

Sooner or later the hunt would take hold of him again and the search he'd started for his little sister would have to go on. Until he'd finished it, one way or the other. His personal guilt for what had happened to

Lara that day made it all but impossible for him to put it to rest once and for all.

He couldn't move on with his life.

He could only keep moving.

She felt his weight shifting slightly beneath her as he stirred, half awake, half asleep. His eyelids were closed, and for the moment he looked oddly peaceful. As if the pain that was always with him had abated for a while. As if their passion had helped him forget, if only for a short time.

His features were relaxed, rugged, his suntanned skin darkly contrasting with the golden waves of his hair. It was the color of beach sand beneath the soft glow of the chandelier. Shifting, moving. Mesmerizing.

The massive strength of his broad chest and shoulders was strangely at odds with the wild, satin sheen of it. That strength had saved her from Gorilla Guy, but in spite of their firmly packed power, the arms that were cradling her now could not protect her from herself. Unlike Armand, Jack had not tried to shelter her. He'd managed to show her herself instead.

Unlike Armand, he could not give her the protection she needed from the past. No reassurances that he would stick around for good. No promises that he would never leave her.

No promises of any sort.

How could she throw her impending marriage away for no more than a single night of pure feeling? How could she trade a pledge of eternal commitment for a few hours of soul-shattering passion?

As the time of reckoning drew closer and the first sounds of daybreak were stirring outside, Eden finally came to terms with some of the questions that were plaguing her. Questions that she did not have the luxury of answering.

Jack had given her no options, no alternatives. There were no choices to make. No promises to break.

There was nothing left to be done but make the ransom drop. And wait with open arms for Armand to be returned to her.

"I want to go with you."

Jack stared at Ed across the long wooden worktable where they'd begun their mad, passionate lovemaking only hours before. A lot could change in a few hours, he realized. That was all the time it had taken for Ms. Eden Wellbourne to turn his entire world upside down.

One night of lovemaking, and he did mean *love* making, and he knew he would never be the same again. She'd bewitched him with her sweet, bare body, beguiled him with her fascinating female favors, seduced him with her irresistibly sexy scent. And then, when she'd had him right where she wanted him, naked, vulnerable, and completely prone, she'd forced him to fall in love with her.

This back room of hers wasn't simply a workshop where she experimented with formulas and fragrances. It was a sultry, steaming hothouse of desire where she concocted her cauldron of devil's brew. Witchcraft, that's what his Princess was practicing, making lotions and potions to drive men mad.

And she was doing a damn good job of it.

They were fully dressed again, preparing to make the drop, and still he couldn't get his mind off her and back on his work where it belonged. He was confused, bewildered, befuddled. What was she saying? That she wanted to be with him? That she'd decided not to marry Herman after all?

"Jack," she said, handing him the tiny vial of formula she'd just sealed inside a plain white envelope, "did you hear me? I want to go with you to deliver this. I want to be there."

His brain cleared quickly, coming suddenly out of the fog. She wanted to *go* with him, not *be* with him. The realization hit him just in time, like a bucket of cold water over the head of a man on fire. He'd been about to make an incredibly idiotic fool of himself by leaping bodily across the table and starting to kiss her senseless again. He'd been about to—what? Go down on one knee in front of her? Propose to a woman who was already engaged?

Not bloody likely. There was no chance in hell of that happening, no matter how strong the love potion she'd poisoned him with. He still wasn't that big a fool.

He had enough coherent gray matter remaining to know that a lady like Ed would never belong to him. Not in his wildest dreams. He didn't deserve to have her.

He would never be free to belong to her.

He took the envelope from her hand, tucked it safely into his shirt pocket. "I do this alone," he said tersely, "or I don't do it at all. It's too dangerous," he added.

Her eyes blinked up at him, widening in fear. "You'll be careful, won't you? You won't let yourself get hurt?"

Too late for that, Princess. "No," he said. "Of course not. Everything's going to be fine." He came around to the other side of the table, took her chin in his hand, gave her shoulders an encouraging little shake. "Just stay put and I'll be back in a flash."

He was out the door before she had a chance to

protest any further. Before the good-byes could get messy.

Before he had a chance to change his mind about delivering her fiancé back to her.

The traffic out front was beginning to pick up as the sun rose higher. Heading for the back alley directly behind Pulse Points, Jack spotted the empty trash cans where he'd been instructed to make the drop.

Whoever the kidnappers were, corporate thieves from Scentsations perfume company or just your run-of-the-mill international scumbags, they'd certainly picked an interesting spot to leave the goods in.

A clever, conveniently deserted spot where there was no decent place for a PI to hide. At the moment, there wasn't another soul anywhere in sight. The alley itself was narrow, long and empty except for a motley collection of unmatched trash containers that the shopkeepers stored out back. At least they were marked, which made it easier to pick the particular can that belonged to Pulse Points.

The kidnappers would have to have cased the joint pretty good to know about that. Then again, maybe they'd been familiar with the layout all along. The theory that the job was an inside one had occurred to him more than once. Maybe orchestrated by someone much closer to Ed than she realized.

The sister? For his Princess's sake, he sure as hell prayed it wasn't her. Still, he doubted that Hope had anything to do with it. She wanted to see Ed happily married even more than Ed did herself.

The father? Not likely. He was a dirtbag to be sure, but Ed hadn't laid eyes on him in years.

The mother had passed away. She had no other family to speak of. And if this whole fiasco really was the work of someone tight with Ed, that only left . . .

A crash sounded fifty feet or so down the alley, distracting him. The lid of a can rattled and fell to the pavement. Something small and furry scurried off into the shadows. A varmint of indeterminate origin.

Jack swore softly, wondering where in the hell he was going to hide his 175-pound frame if an animal the size of a squirrel couldn't sneak around without being spotted. Still, he couldn't waste any more time waiting. He had to make the move now, before anyone showed up.

Casually he lifted the lid on the Pulse Points container, carelessly slipping the envelope inside. Next he put his homegrown Florida brain to work and came up with a spur-of-the-moment place to hang out in while he waited. The Dumpster twenty feet down the way. Not exactly five-star accommodations, but a man had to make do with what he had.

As he slipped over the edge of the reeking, stinking container, reluctantly settling himself inside, he didn't miss the awful irony of the situation. He'd believed he was trash for most of his life. He was finally proving himself right.

Selecting a spot in the metal wall that was somewhere near eye level, he rubbed away at the rust until a peephole appeared. He put his face to the opening, testing the view. Not bad for a quick, slapdash job.

Ten minutes later he was still staring out into the deserted, half-dark alleyway, impatiently waiting for his date to show up.

Trapped as he was now, with nothing else to occupy him, he had no choice but to own up to the simple, undeniable fact that he'd broken his own rule, big time.

He'd gone so far beyond personal involvement with a client, it wasn't even close to stepping over the line.

It was more like he'd stepped off a cliff.

God, but what a fool he was.

He'd fallen in love with Ed Wellbourne.

He'd thought he wasn't capable of that particular emotion any longer. He'd thought he couldn't love anything but his own independence, the freedom to keep moving when and where he needed to for the sake of the hunt. He had believed he couldn't love anyone but Lara.

He'd been wrong.

Aw hell, *love*.

The four-letter word. The ultimate agony. It was the one lethal emotion he'd been running from his entire adult life, and this time it really was going to kill him. He was going to have to hand Herman back to her.

And then he was going to die.

He didn't even have to think about doing himself in with a weapon. Ed was going to pull the trigger personally when she went ahead and married that sniveling French schmuck.

His Princess was going to fire the fatal shot into him all by herself.

Still scanning the alley, he felt an insanity come over him, an emotion so strong and unfamiliar he had no hope of naming it immediately. The only hope he had at the moment was the overwhelming desire to see Herman show up. *In a body bag*, he thought ruthlessly, *or not at all*.

It was jealousy, Jack realized. Insane, stark raving jealousy. Hell, but he just couldn't handle the thought that the geek was going to have his Princess for life.

Forever.

In the end, he knew, the goon was going to get her.

Because that's the way the world worked. Because that's what she'd wanted all along. The cold, clinical chemist was going to show up, alive and well, and then he was going to put his hands all over Ed. The creep. The schmoe.

The lucky, stinking bastard.

Jack was just beginning to imagine how many ways there were to strangle a man, slowly, when a strange noise sounded from the front of the shop. A faint noise that didn't belong against the background of distant traffic. A bell? A whistle? He closed his eyes, straining to hear the odd, high-pitched note, when a second noise sounded.

A scream.

Ed's scream.

It tore through him, ripped his insides apart. He was out of the Dumpster in seconds, racing for the front entrance of Pulse Points, running as fast as he'd ever moved in his life.

If anything had happened to her, he would never forgive himself.

It was his worst nightmare happening all over again. The person he loved was in need of him, in trouble, and he was momentarily helpless to save her.

He rounded the corner, his heart in his throat, his blood pounding painfully in his ears. He saw her. *Oh, God, thank God, he saw her.*

Better yet, she seemed to be okay. She was running herself, dashing around the opposite corner of the shop. Jack's legs were so weak with relief, he could barely move them. Regardless, he continued to follow her at warp speed.

What the hell was going on? His first thought was that his Princess was running away from someone.

Catching up with her seconds later, he realized she'd been running *after* someone instead.

Babette.

She'd been chasing the poodle, who had somehow escaped from the confines of the store. Ed was fine, although a little shaken up as she grabbed for the dog and scooped her up in her arms, hugging and scolding her all at the same time.

It was exactly what Jack wanted to do to his Princess just then. Scold her. Hug her.

Then never let her go.

"Ed," he demanded, "what happened?"

She was holding Babette so protectively that the little dog's head was barely visible from the crook of her arm. "It all happened so fast," she said. "I heard a whistle outside. I didn't think anything of it, at first. I was still in the back room, waiting, when I realized that Babette had heard the sound too. I heard her scratching at the bathroom window, trying to get out. When I made it to the bathroom myself, she *was* out. The screen was gone and so was she."

"And that's when you screamed?"

She nodded. "I'm sorry. I couldn't help it. I was so terrified for her."

Jack couldn't blame her. He understood all too well how she'd felt.

"Then I found her out here," Ed said, "scratching and pawing at the ground as if she'd caught the scent of something."

Jack surveyed the spot where Babette had been found. If anything had been there, anything or *anyone*, they had done a pretty quick disappearing act. The window screen still lay by the side of the building where it had fallen. Correction, where it had been *pushed* to the ground.

A screen that looked far too big for a three-pound dog to have dislodged from the window frame.

"Ed," he told her, "get back inside with Babette. I'll be right there."

If his hunch was right, he'd only be a few moments. In fact, he didn't even have to make the short trip back to the deserted alley to know that the vial of perfume he'd left in the garbage can was already long gone. He did check it out anyway, just to physically confirm what he'd figured out mentally.

The envelope was missing. The perpetrators had made off with it during all the commotion. How convenient for them. How coincidental that such a distraction had occurred at just the right time.

How completely he'd fallen for their setup.

He hadn't been able to help himself. He'd fallen for the trick just as completely as he'd fallen in love with Ed. Without thinking. Without a heartbeat's worth of time to consider the consequences.

Damn, but he was a fool in more ways than one.

By the time he reentered the shop, Ed was already talking on the phone. Judging by the happy, high-pitched tone of her voice, he had a pretty damn good idea who it was. Herman. So his stupid blunder hadn't gotten the guy killed after all.

Too bad, he thought viciously. *Too bloody bad.*

"It's Armand," she whispered, her hand over the mouthpiece. "He's been released! He's all right."

"That's great," he lied. "Just great."

She finished the short conversation, replaced the receiver. "He's on his way," she said, breathless. "The kidnappers dropped him off half a mile from here. Within walking distance of the shop."

"Well," Jack managed to say, "that's convenient."

He didn't want to point out the possibility the whole scenario might've been just a little too convenient. He had no definite proof that anything more sinister than a simple kidnapping had occurred. What right did he have to burst her bubble, anyway? What reason beyond pure selfishness on his part?

There was only one thing he wanted to know now. Only one thing he needed to know. *What was she going to do next?*

Still, he couldn't bring himself to ask. He didn't have to ask. The answer was already written clearly across her beautifully flushed face.

She was going to welcome Armand home with open arms.

The realization stunned him, slammed through his stinking, sore body with a brutality he should've been prepared for. He wasn't, even though he'd seen it coming all along. It was time to do his job, he reminded himself harshly. The one she'd hired him to perform in the first place.

Time to give Ed back her dream.

And the only way he could bring himself to do that was by disappearing from her life for good. Now, right now, before the happy reunion could get under way.

He wasn't going to stick around long enough to watch that scenario.

No, he wasn't going to hang around to meet the geeky bastard and witness a sight that was bound to make him sick. He was going to get the hell out of here before Ed had the chance to hand him his walking papers.

A muscle worked in his jaw. "Tell you what, Princess," he said, "I'm going to make myself scarce."

The flush left her face as her skin went suddenly pale. "You're leaving? Just like that?"

He shrugged, congratulating himself for how cool and calm he sounded when all he really wanted to do was ransack the room and make off with her on the back of his bike. "You know what they say, Ed. Two's company, three's a crowd. Well, I'm going to get out of here before the place gets a little too crowded."

"Jack—"

"Don't, Princess. We both knew it had to end sooner or later."

Tears sprang to her eyes. Jack swore fiercely under his breath. How much was one man supposed to handle? He didn't think he could take it if she started crying on him. Not now.

"Jack, I don't know how I can ever thank you enough for everything you've done."

He wasn't sure if it was pain he read on her face or pity. God, pity. He could take anything from her but that.

His laugh was harsh. Aw, hell, he really was starting to lose it. "Don't worry, Ms. Wellbourne. I'll send you my bill."

She winced at the words. "*Jack*—"

But he wasn't listening any longer. There was no use in prolonging the inevitable. No sense in putting off the pain. He brushed past her into the back room, retrieved his helmet and the stack of envelopes, making sure he hadn't left anything lying around.

Nope, he reassured himself. Nothing but his heart.

With a quick farewell swipe across the top of Babette's furry head, he was out the front door.

The motorcycle roared to life beneath him. He pulled out into the street, gunned the engine, took off down the road without bothering to look back.

It was good to be traveling again, he told himself fiercely. There were worse things in life than losing the woman you loved. At the moment, though, he just couldn't think of them.

Still, there were things to be grateful for. He hadn't made a complete blubbering fool of himself, only a partial one. He hadn't hung around and begged. He'd ended it himself. Cleanly. Quickly.

If a man had to cut his own heart out, that was definitely the way to do it. Nice and neat. At least he could take comfort in the fact that he'd done the deed at all.

Yeah, that definitely made him feel so much better. He'd remembered his mission statement at the time it mattered the most. Remembered the words he'd learned to live by for so long.

An unhappy ending was better than no ending at all.

TWELVE

"It's here," Hope said, her voice hushed, almost reverent as she carried a white garment bag into the back room of the shop and carefully hooked the hanger over the back of the door. "The dress. It's finally arrived."

Eden glanced up from the scent organ, where she'd been pretending to work for the past few hours. Only she hadn't been working. She hadn't been able to compose anything for nearly a week.

Not since the day Jack Rafferty had taken off.

The long vinyl bag looked ominous hanging there. Like a great white ghost that had just floated into the room. She gazed at it, inexplicably frightened by the strangely eerie sight.

"Well?" Hope prompted. "Aren't you going to try it on?"

"I'm sure it's fine," she said, shaking her head. "I'll put it on later."

"You'll put it on now," her sister said sternly, "or the seamstress at the shop will personally have my head on a platter. She's spent a week on the alterations already, and if you need any more pinning and tucking done by Saturday, it's going to be too late."

"Okay, okay," Eden told her, reluctantly giving in, "but only for you, not for that sadistic seamstress at the bridal store. I'm tired of being poked and pierced by that cruel woman. She's cut and sewn me over so many times, I'm beginning to feel like the Bride of Frankenstein."

The laugh she let out was slightly hysterical. First she'd been imagining ghosts and now she was dreaming up ghouls. Her subconscious mind was going a little crazy from all the prewedding stress. Of course, she didn't think of Armand as the wicked Dr. Frankenstein.

Not even the traumatic stress of the kidnapping had changed his usual behavior. He still wanted to marry her as much as ever.

"Eden, honey," her sister said kindly, "I know your nerves are on edge right now, but you're the one who asked for all the alterations in the first place. I thought you liked the design when we first picked it out. Aren't you happy with it now?"

Shrugging, Eden stood up, ditched her shirt, and let her sister slip the long white garment over her head. Gathering up the train, she walked to the bathroom, checking her image out in the full-length door mirror.

Was she happy with it?

She hated it. It was undoubtedly the most ghastly gathering of sophisticated satin, stiff, formal lace, and simple seed pearls she'd ever seen in her life. How could she have ever chosen such a thing? High-collared, long-sleeved, with a train the length of a church aisle. It was stuffy, understated, elegant.

It was slowly choking the life out of her.

Hope stood behind her, tears in her eyes. Tears of joy, Eden realized.

"I love it," she lied.

"It's beautiful," Hope said. "Just beautiful."

Babette apparently did not agree with her sister's generous pronouncement. The poodle jumped down from her new favorite spot on the chaise lounge, where she'd been camped out for the past several days, and barked fiercely at the swishing, shimmering length of long white skirt.

"Settle down," Eden said. "It's okay."

Babette didn't listen. Something about the dress still seemed to be bothering her. In fact, something had been bothering the dog for days. Ever since Armand had returned . . .

"Poor little thing," Hope said, picking her up, trying to soothe her. "What's the matter, baby Babette? Did a ghost just walk across your grave?"

"A ghost?"

"Oh, you know what I mean. She's been barking at shadows for days. Acting funny. If I didn't know better, I'd say she's pouting. Do you think she might be getting sick?"

Eden couldn't deny that Babette had been behaving strangely. But she did have a pretty good idea what was affecting her pooch, and it definitely wasn't illness. It was the same thing that had been bothering her for the past week. The thing that had been haunting them both.

It wasn't a ghost.

It was the memory of Jack Rafferty.

He was still here, in this room, where they'd spent that one night together. His scent still lingered faintly, seductively on the cotton fabric covering the chaise lounge. It clung to the pillows, whispered along the length of the down-filled cushion. That smell was the reason the poodle had selected the chaise as her favorite new resting spot.

She was in mourning for her adored pack leader who had suddenly disappeared without warning. She missed him.

Eden had to admit, she missed him, too.

But there was no sign that she would ever see him again. No clue that he had any intention of ever returning to her.

Was that what she was hoping for? That he would suddenly appear, sweep her happily off her feet, and carry her away to live with him forever? That he would sail off into the sunset with her on his rickety old houseboat? That wasn't what she wanted.

Was it?

"Babette's going to be fine," she said to Hope. "We all are as soon as this wedding is over."

"Of course you are," her sister agreed, dropping Babette back onto the chaise and coming back again to study her reflection in the mirror. "Now, have you decided how you're going to wear your hair?"

"Up, *certainement*," a cool male voice sounded behind her. "You should wear it up and neatly pinned, chignon style. That gown is far too gorgeous, too *couture* to let anything detract from it."

She turned to see her fiancé standing in the doorway. Dark haired and Gallic, he smiled his admiration at her chic choice of wedding gown. "You will certainly do the Guillon family proud, *ma chère*," he added approvingly.

"Armand!" she exclaimed, inexplicably annoyed, "I didn't hear you come in. You shouldn't be here, you know."

"She's right," Hope added, scolding him. "Don't you know it's bad luck for you to see the dress before the wedding day?"

"With a bride this lovely," he said, stepping forward to place two ceremonial kisses on either side of Eden's face, "who requires luck?"

Watching his movements from the vantage point of the chaise, Babette lifted her head at him, growling.

"It seems I have not one, but all three females angry with me," he joked lightly. "Darling, would you prefer that I leave?"

"No, I—of course not. I'm glad to see you. There are a few last-minute details we still need to talk about."

"Guess that's my cue," Hope said, "to leave you two lovebirds alone. Come on, Babette, baby, let's go mind the store."

The poodle continued growling in a low, agitated tone as Hope carried her past them and disappeared into the front room.

"Perhaps I should buy you a cat for a wedding present," Armand joked again. "A fifteen-pounder, no? *Le grand chat pour la chienne méchante.*"

"She'll get used to you," Eden promised, ignoring the joke, "eventually."

"*C'est possible,*" he agreed. "Anything's possible. Now, what are the details you wished to discuss with me?"

Eden let out a deep breath, then rattled off a long list of minor etiquette questions she'd been storing in her mind. Armand was a stickler for that sort of thing, and she didn't want to make any embarrassing cultural *faux pas* in front of his friends and family.

He let out a long whistle when she was finally finished. "My darling, it sounds as if your worries are end-less."

A shivering chill snaked suddenly down Eden's spine. Not at Armand's all-too-true, premonitory words, but at the sound he'd just made. The high-pitched whistle. It was eerie, frighteningly familiar. Where had she recently heard it?

"Darling?" he asked, "Is something troubling you?"

She nodded, swallowing hard. "Armand," she began, "I know you'd prefer not to talk about what happened—the kidnapping—because it must have been traumatic for you, but I do need to discuss it. I need to tell you something. I have a confession to make."

"A confession, *ma chère*?" he asked, smiling. "Is this the dramatic moment when you admit to me that you have been unfaithful and known another man?"

"Yes," she said, "it is. I have."

The cool smile never left his face. "But darling, this is not as surprising to me as you may imagine. You are a lovely, desirable woman, and we are still unmarried. What happens before the wedding vows is not as sacro-sanct as what occurs afterward. In fact, it is something of a continental tradition in my country to continue to take lovers throughout the marriage, so you see, I am not shocked."

He wasn't surprised at all, she realized. But he should have been. It was almost as if he had known, somehow, as if he had been somewhere close by that fateful week, watching her and Jack. At The Jungle, es-pecially, when they'd made such a point of showing public affection.

It was almost as if he had been there.

"So, you don't mind, then?" she asked.

He shrugged. "Would you prefer that I fly into a jealous rage?"

Yes, she thought wildly. She would prefer anything to his chilling, detached calmness. "I—I don't know what I was expecting. I just wanted to tell you so we wouldn't start off our marriage with any secrets between us."

"And so, you would wish me to share mine with you as well?"

Another warning whistle went off inside her head. *Be careful what you wish for.*

She nodded. "I want you to tell me everything."

And then, to her horror, he did.

Jack staggered home from Lizard's Lounge, weaving his way gradually back to the boat through the early morning mist. A dry bed and a long nap were the only things on his mind at the moment, which meant he'd successfully accomplished what he'd set out to do the night before. Get *her* out of his mind.

It hadn't been easy. It had taken several drinks before the brilliant plan had even begun to work. After that, the evening had passed by in a merciful blur, the same way every night had floated by him this week. In a dazed, drunken dream. A dream that kept the nightmare of reality away.

A muscle throbbed in his forehead, pounding, pulsating. He rubbed the spot gingerly, trying to remember why it was aching so. Of course, the fact that he was hard up and hurting with a one-hundred-proof hangover was cause enough to make his head ache, but through the haze he struggled to recall the true reason.

Oh, yeah. The beer-can-crushing contest he'd chal-

lenged Bones to. Another one of his genius ideas. The
object had been to smash aluminum cans against your
forehead, accordion style. The purpose had been to de-
termine which one of them had a thicker, stupider,
more stubborn head.

He'd won.

Finally reaching his front porch, he wobbled inside,
dropped to the couch, and closed his eyes, welcoming
the whirling, hideous pain. He didn't want it to stop. He
wanted it to go on and on, blocking out everything else.
Blocking out the memories of Ed. That's all Ms.
Wellbourne was to him at this moment.

One massive ache in his brain.

Somewhere in the sickening fog he heard a noise. A
knock.

He groaned, ignoring it. Maybe it would go away.

It didn't.

"Get lost," he said. "There's no one home."

"Jack Rafferty?" A voice asked from outside.

A female voice, but definitely not Ed's. He promised
himself he was glad it wasn't Ed's. He was thrilled. If he
could only get this cruelly determined person to go
away, his life would be complete.

There was only one way to do that, he realized. He
stood, staggered toward the door, and flung it open,
determined to shut it in Ms. Persistent Female's face
again. It was what he should have done with Ms.
Wellbourne. It was what he was going to do with this
woman. He glared down at her in open annoyance. Just
what he needed. Another stubborn, feisty female.

He was just about to bark out at her and tell her to
take a long hike off a short pier, when something in her
small, grinning face stopped him. Something familiar.

Her expression was amused, almost mischievous. Was it . . .

No. His mind was playing tricks on him. He was hallucinating, imagining things in the middle of his beer-induced stupor.

"Jack?" she asked, seeming to recognize him.

Her face swam before him. He blinked again and the incredible vision slowly cleared. "Lara?"

"Feeling better?"

Jack found himself seated on his couch, staring in shock at the fresh, lively features of a young woman he'd never expected to see again. Lara. She was alive. She was here with him in his house.

The vision began to blur a bit as the hangover took hold of him. He closed his eyes again, groaning, then reluctantly blinked them open. She was still there. Still smiling over at him. This couldn't be real.

"I'm dead, aren't I?" he demanded.

She laughed. "You should be, judging by how awful you look. And smell. I'm not even sure I should be so happy I found you."

"How did you find me?" he asked.

"I saw my picture on a poster in the office where I work. I thought someone was playing a joke on me. I didn't even know I was missing."

Jack hung his head in his hands, trying to comprehend what she was saying.

"I didn't even think you were alive," she added. "Dad told me you and mom were both dead."

"Dad?" he repeated, his head jerking up. "You've been with him all this time?"

She shook her head slowly and continued to explain. "He passed away a long time ago. When I was ten."

"That bastard stole you?" he said bluntly.

She nodded. "I guess he did, although I didn't realize it at the time. Like I said, he led me to believe that you and mom were gone. I thought he was all the family I had left."

"Jesus, Lara. I've been looking for you forever. How in the hell did he hide you? How in the hell did he get away with it?"

"Jack, I'm so sorry." She took his large hand in her small one, squeezed it hard. "I think—well, do you remember what a tomboy I was? I think that's how he did it. He took me out of school, made me cook for him, clean for him. But whenever we went out in public, he passed me off as a boy."

He groaned. "So the whole time I was looking for a girl . . . Jesus, Lara."

"It's my fault that bastard stole you. I should never have left you alone."

She squeezed his hand again, harder. "Of course it wasn't your fault. If it makes you feel any better, things got better for me after he was gone. The state placed me in foster care and I was lucky enough to get adopted by a great family. I'm married now, with a little girl of my own."

Jack choked back a mix of emotions he couldn't begin to manage all at once. Emotions he hadn't let himself feel in years. Overwhelming relief. The release of an enormous weight being lifted off his shoulders. A soaring sense of deep joy.

Protective, powerful, brotherly love. For the first time in his life it didn't hurt him any longer.

He tried to swallow back the sound that rose inside

him, but it wasn't any use. He was crying, weeping as he had never wept in his life. Lara seemed to understand what he was feeling. She put her arms around him then and hugged him hard.

"Thank you," she said against his shoulder, "for never giving up."

He nodded, pulled back to compose himself.

"Enough about my life for the moment," she went on. "Tell me something about yours."

"What life?" he joked. "You're looking at it. I'm a PI. Single."

"Single? You're kidding. You're too handsome for that."

"Right. As you can see, there is a long line of women lined up at my door, just dying to marry me. Go out there with a stick and beat them back for me, would you?"

"Well, you'd be even more handsome if you didn't look like you'd been out all night, raising hell. My guess is, you don't do it that often, though."

"What makes you say that?"

She punched him playfully in the gut. "Simple. No beer belly."

He grinned. "Go easy there, little sister. Not only have I been out all night raising hell, but I'm nursing the mother of all hangovers."

"Interesting," Lara mused. "Who is she?"

"Excuse me?"

"The woman who's done this to you. Who is she?"

"No one."

"I knew it. There's always a woman. Tell me about her."

"God, are you always this nosy?"

"Usually I'm worse. Now, give. Spill the beans. Are you madly in love with her?"

Jack couldn't help laughing. This kind of relationship was all new to him. He wasn't used to sharing personal information with a family member. Wasn't used to trusting anyone. But his camaraderie with Lara was instinctive. It wasn't long before he found himself admitting the awful truth to her.

"Yeah," he said, "I'm madly in love with her."

"So what's the problem, then?"

"She's almost married to another man."

"Almost married? That's like saying she's almost won the lottery. Either she has or she hasn't."

"She hasn't. But she's going to sometime tomorrow."

"Tomorrow, huh?" she mused. "That still gives you *plenty* of time to go after her."

"No way," Jack said. "She's made her choice."

"She's told you she doesn't want to marry you, then?"

"Well—no. I haven't actually asked her."

"What! But you've at least told her that you love her, right?"

"Well, no, I haven't done that either."

"*Men*," she said in disgust. "It's a good thing I showed up here when I did."

"I'm beginning to wonder about that," Jack muttered in wry amusement.

"Brother," Lara said, "do you need my help."

Eden had just placed the Closed sign in the front window of Pulse Points when she heard it. A motorcycle, judging by the sound of it. She glanced down the street, her heart in her throat.

It's not him, she told herself. It's never going to be him. But it was.

As she watched through the window, Jack Rafferty pulled up on his motorcycle, roaring to a stop directly in front of the store. He's probably just come to collect his payment, she warned herself, swallowing hard.

He cut the engine, swung his leg over the side, booted the kickstand into position against the pavement. When the helmet came off, Eden's breath caught at the sight of him. God, but he was gorgeous, cool and confident, ruggedly beautiful.

Ought to have a scent named after him. No, an aftershave. It would come in a solid steel bottle, for the customer's own safety. *Eau de Heartbreaker.* The stuff would fly off the shelves.

Purposefully he left the bike behind, strolled toward the entrance of the shop, and firmly pounded his fist against the rattling front door. Babette went ballistic at the sound of it, jumping and pawing at the inside of the door, crying to get out. To get to him.

"Open up, Ed. I know you're in there."

Eden scooped the poodle up in her arms, attempting to calm her. "Shameless pooch," she whispered, "have you no pride? He walked out on us, remember? Left us flat the moment his mission was over."

"Princess," Jack said, "unlock this door. Now."

"The check's in the mail," she said, hoping to discourage him.

"That's my line, love. It won't work, anyway. Now, are you going to open this door, or do I have to break it down?"

She didn't doubt he was capable of it. But it wasn't

the threat of impending property damage that really riveted her attention. It was that word he'd used. Love.

Was it simply a slip of the tongue or something more? Either way, she had little choice but to let him in. Thank goodness.

She turned the lock, stepped back as he pushed his way inside. Babette went bonkers.

"Hey, Babs," he said affectionately, stooping momentarily to fluff the bouncing, springing, leaping top of her head. "Now, settle down," he added firmly, standing again to face Eden. "Go take a short doggie snooze. Your mistress and I need to talk uninterrupted."

To Eden's consternation Babette instantly obeyed, strutting happily over to her corner pillow and curling up into a contented bagel.

"What is it you'd like to talk about?" she asked, hoping that her feigned politeness would mask the fear rising inside her.

The fear that she would run forward, fling her arms around Rafferty's broad chest, and beg him to never leave her again. She tried to promise herself that wasn't going to happen, but she knew by now what empty promises were worth. Nothing. There were no guarantees any longer. No safety net for her to fall back on.

"This is about you and me, Ed, but I think you know that by now. I'm here to talk about us."

"There isn't any us," she insisted. "There can't be."

"There can if you give me a little more time to convince you you're making a mistake, Ed. Princess, I want you to postpone the wedding."

She drew in a deep breath, shaking her head. "Somehow I don't think that's going to be necessary."

Jack swore softly, folded his arms across his chest, began pacing back and forth across the showroom floor.

"Stubborn as usual," he muttered. "That's it, then, Ed. You're leaving me no choice. There's only one thing left to do." He came toward her, took her in his arms.

"First," he explained, in his languid Southern drawl, "I'm going to make love to you until you can't breathe any longer." He flashed a cool and cocky grin. "And then I'm going to have to murder Herman."

Eden blinked up at him, not entirely sure if he was joking or not. "Stand in line," she said, "because my sister, Hope, might beat you to it."

He frowned down at her. "Ed, has he done something to hurt you? Where is the sniveling bastard, anyway?"

"Somewhere over the Atlantic by now," she told him. "On his way back to France."

Jack blinked at her in shock. "Princess, you'd better tell me what happened."

She put her hands to her eyes, closing them momentarily as she wondered what part she should share with him first. The betrayal, the embarrassment, her own stupidity. It was all so awful she didn't know where to start.

"First of all," she said, "I broke it off. There isn't going to be any wedding. Armand did something horrible, something I couldn't live with. I thought he was so smart!" she said bitterly. "And he was brilliant all right. He put together a brilliant plan and made me a part of it without telling me. He lied to me, almost from the start. *He engineered the whole thing.*"

"Whoa, Princess, slow down a little. Take a deep breath and tell me exactly what he did. And *then* I'm going to kill him."

"He faked it," she said, "everything. The disappearance, the break-in, the ransom note. Right down to the color of the stationery he used because he knew that I would recognize it and suspect Scentsations. Only they didn't do it. There was never any kidnapping."

Jack nodded at her, slowly. "I suspected he might've had a hand in it."

"What? Why didn't you say something?"

"I didn't have any proof, Princess. Would you have believed me, anyway? Were you ready to hear it?"

"I—no. I don't know."

"It was the motive that stumped me," he said. "I couldn't quite put my finger on *why* he would do it. The bastard had everything, as far as I could see."

"It was greed," she explained in disgust. "Simple, selfish greed. Scentsations wasn't trying to steal the formula, Armand was trying to *sell* it to them for cash. But he had to make it look like a corporate theft so the House of Guillon management wouldn't figure out what he was doing. He hired a couple of thugs to ransack the shop, but when they couldn't find the document with my half of the formula on it . . ."

"He was forced to fake his own kidnapping."

"Exactly. He actually felt he deserved the millions Scentsations would pay him because his scientific work went unrewarded at Guillon. His dad held the purse strings and never gave him the credit. He saw the new scent as his ticket to wealth and independence from his father's control."

"Poor bastard. I wonder *how* I should kill him."

"Jack," she said, "you still haven't heard the worst part."

"Ed," he promised her, "nothing could be worse than the thought of you marrying that man. Tell me the rest."

"It's about the scent," she said, "the new formula

Armand was so proud of. He experimented with it after we'd created the base composition together. He added some very unusual ingredients to it. Synthetic pheromones."

He frowned at her. "Pheromones? I'm no scientist, Ed, but isn't that the stuff that bugs use to attract each other with?"

She nodded. "Precisely. It's a combination of chemicals so powerful that insects can detect the opposite sex from miles away. It's a kind of scent hormone that animals produce for one purpose only. *Mating.*"

"Sounds interesting. But why in hell would Armand put bug attractants in perfume?"

"He didn't use insect pheromones," she said solemnly. "He used human ones. Man-woman attractants."

Jack whistled softly. He put a hand to his chin, rubbing thoughtfully across the freshly shaved surface. "So, let me get this straight. The new scent is more than just perfume. In fact," he went on, "it was specifically formulated to attract the opposite sex. Which makes it a—"

"*Love potion.*"

"Princess," he said, "that's impossible."

Eden shook her head sadly. "I thought so too. At first. Some scientists aren't even sure if pheromones actually exist in humans, but Armand swore that he isolated the compounds in the laboratory. Synthesized and tested them too."

"Tested them on what? Some unfortunate guinea pig?"

She inclined her head slowly, attempting a smile. "You're looking at her."

"That dirtball, he wouldn't—"

"I'm afraid he did. Now I know why he didn't argue about adopting out all the lab animals. They weren't useful to him any longer. He needed a human to continue his experiment with. Me."

"His death will be slow," Jack promised. "Slow and excruciatingly painful."

"He presented me with the vial on our first date. It's absorbed through the skin. I dabbed some on myself. He had secretly applied some to himself earlier. Apparently, both subjects have to be wearing it. Well, he could hardly believe the results himself. He says the fact that I fell for him and agreed to marry him was the best proof of all how well the stuff worked."

Jack's laugh was harsh, disbelieving. "The geek's got that part right. Nothing short of a scientific miracle would make him good enough for you to get engaged to. But Ed, you're *not* going to marry him. So it doesn't really work after all. You don't love him. You never did."

"That's the problem!" she exclaimed. "I don't know. I thought I was in love with him, but then . . ." She swallowed hard, hesitating. "Then I met you."

He came toward her again and Eden felt something breaking down inside her. The glass walls were shattering. Deep emotions were spilling out all around her. She couldn't keep her feelings bottled up any longer.

"And then?" Jack said, taking her by the shoulders and giving them an urgent little shake. "Tell me what happened next, Princess. I need to hear it. You have no idea how badly."

Her heart squeezed tight as she looked into his eyes, then swelled and expanded, overflowing. "You want me to say it?" she asked, a little desperate, a little crazed from the overwhelming emotions she felt swirling around her. "All right. I will. I fell in love with you," she admitted, nearly sobbing on the words, they were that hard to get out. "I'll say it again if you want, although I can hardly believe it myself. *I fell in love with you.*"

Jack's whole body seemed to shudder with one heavy sigh of relief as he looked down at her. He didn't say anything for a very long time. Nothing.

To Eden the hesitation was like an eternity. Well, she thought, how nice. How perfectly peachy her life was at this moment. She'd already been betrayed by one man this week, called off her wedding, and now she'd just made a total idiot of herself in front of another. But what Armand had done to her heart was nothing compared to Jack's terrible silence.

"Are you happy now?" she added crossly. "My humiliation is complete."

His laugh was low and lazy, more relaxed than she'd ever seen it, his grin was sexier than sin. "Yeah," he admitted. "I'm happy. So happy, I could kiss you, Princess. But I won't. Yet. First I'm going to tell you that I love you back. I do, Ed. Completely."

Eden's heart had ached so badly to hear those words, it nearly burst now from the sound of them. "That's awful," she said, the tears springing to her eyes. "Bad news. Really terrible."

Jack's grin grew even wider as he took her into his arms and hugged her tight. "I thought so too," he whispered in her ear, "until I learned that love doesn't have to hurt. You taught me that, Ed."

"I did?" she breathed in amazement, pulling back to look at him.

He brushed a tear from her cheek. "Uh-huh. You and another young woman I've been talking to recently. Lara."

"Lara?" She sniffed as the name slowly sunk in. "Jack, you found her!"

He nodded, hugging her nearly off her feet this time. "Because of you, baby. The new reward posters did their trick."

"Jack," she said when he finally set her down again, "that's so wonderful. I'm so happy for you. I hope I can meet her someday."

He laughed. "I don't think she's going to settle for someday, Princess. She wants an introduction yesterday. And she's not the sort of lady it's easy to say no to."

Eden's eyebrows went up in amusement. "Oh, really? No doubt it runs in the family."

"No doubt," he agreed, grinning. "She's already making plans for the wedding."

Eden's heart thumped hard against her chest. "Oh! The wedding? Well, if she's getting married, we should introduce her to Hope and the two of them should have a marvelous time planning to their hearts' content. You see, Hope is so disappointed that I called my engagement off and—"

"Lara's already happily married, Ed. Has a baby girl too."

"Oh. How—how nice for her."

"Don't you want to know who's wedding it is she's planning?"

"No!" she exclaimed, ducking her head against his chest. "I don't!"

"Princess," he said, stroking his hand against her hair, her back, "you have to own up to it sooner or later, the same way you've handled everything else. Face the facts, Ms. Wellbourne. We were made for each other."

"No. There's been some mistake."

"Uh-uh," he went on. "I'm going to marry you, Ed.

The sooner the better. And you're going to marry me back."

She pulled back again, sniffing. "You're going to break my heart, aren't you?"

"Never," he promised.

"You'll get tired of it all. You'll get bored and move on."

"Just try and get rid of me."

"We don't have anything in common," she said.

"I can think of at least *one* thing."

"Oh," she murmured, "*that.*"

"This," Jack agreed as he covered his mouth with hers.

"Say yes," he urged, his lips against hers. "Marry me and make me the happiest man alive."

He was serious, she realized. He really meant for them to make a life together, to live happily ever after. He was free to commit to her now that his sister had been found. He'd said it himself. Love didn't hurt him any longer.

She put her hands against his chest, reluctantly pushing him back to arm's length.

"Yes," she said, looking deep into his eyes. "I'll marry you."

Jack couldn't quite believe what he'd heard. He held her again, just stood there and cradled her in his arms for the longest time, until the reality of their happiness really started sinking in. It filled him up as nothing else ever had. He didn't care any longer if he deserved it or not. He *needed* it. God, yes, how much he needed her!

"Princess," he said, finally letting go, but still not letting her go far. "I want to give you everything. My breath. My body . . ."

"Your worldly possessions?" she teased.

"Those too."

"I think I'm going to like living on a houseboat," she informed him. "Luckily, I don't have a lot of furniture. My Paris apartment was pretty small, so I'm sure we'll adjust, as long as you don't mind Country French."

"Actually," he said, "I've developed a distinct distaste for anything from France. I was thinking more along the lines of a simple Florida-style house. Clean lines, lots of fresh air blowing through it, with a shiny tin roof that chimes nice and soft when it rains."

"Sounds heavenly. Peaceful. But I'm afraid we won't be able to afford it for a while. Even though I have half the store, I'm out of a job, remember? And you still have those vet bills, don't you?"

"As a matter of fact, Princess, I decided to pay them off."

"Oh. Did you get a new case?"

"No, just solved an old one. A very old one. There was a substantial reward offered and I was lucky enough to collect on it."

"Great! So, it's enough for a down payment on that house?"

"Ed, the reward money. Every penny I've ever made has gone into that fund. It's been waiting in the bank for fifteen years, compounded daily with a pretty decent rate of return."

She blinked up at him, still half in shock. "What are you saying?"

"That there's enough in that account to buy you a half dozen houses if you want them."

She shook her head in amazement. "One will do nicely, thank you very much." Another thought struck her. "Maybe we should offer the reward to Lara. After all, she did help find herself."

"I've already tried," he said, kissing the top of her head for the unselfish idea. "She won't hear of it."

Seeming to sense the importance of the moment, Babette sat up on her pillow, barking, determined to make herself a part of it.

Jack laughed softly, looking down at the little dog. "I suppose you think we should spend it all on you? Pearl collars and hamburger for dinner every day?"

The poodle barked again in agreement.

"Just like your mistress," he said, grinning at Ed. "Stubborn. Sweet, Determined to get your way."

Her chin went up defiantly, but she couldn't stay angry with him for long. "I suppose it's true," she said, laughing. "Only I didn't get what I bargained for. There are still several hundred embossed dinner napkins that I have no idea what I'm going to do with. Not to mention a year's supply of after-dinner mints."

"Disappointed you didn't have that big church wedding?"

"Never!" she assured him, shuddering. "Promise me that we'll elope. And you'll wear these," she said smiling, tugging on the back of his blue jeans.

"I'll promise you anything, Princess."

"I'd like to keep working," she added, "maybe start my own line of natural fragrances. And maybe have a few kids?" she asked, glancing up at him almost shyly.

"Why don't we get started?" He caught her up in his arms, carried her into the back room.

"Here?" she laughed. "Now?"

"You know how it is with me, Princess. When I start on a mission, I don't give up until I've fulfilled it."

He laid her down on the chaise and proceeded to kiss her senseless.

"Only . . . Jack," she said when they finally came

up for air, "there's still something that's bothering me. It's the new scent. The love potion."

He stopped momentarily to look at her. "Hmm?"

"Well," she went on, hesitantly, "you don't suppose it had anything to do with *us* and our lovemaking, do you? Remember, how I spilled it when—well, you do remember, don't you?"

"Princess," he said, "I'll never forget a second of that night."

"But what if the scent was the reason that I—what if it was all just a chemical reaction to the pheromones?"

"It was a chemical reaction all right," he agreed, "a nuclear reaction. To each other. That potion didn't have a damn thing to do with it."

"Are you sure?"

He put a hand to his chin, rubbing thoughtfully. "Sure I'm sure, Princess, but if you really want proof, I'd suggest an experiment."

"An experiment?"

"Uh-huh," he told her seriously. "A bold clinical trial. It's the only way to find out for certain. We have to do it all over again, this time without the potion, just to make sure."

She looked up at him, smiling sensually. "I see."

"For the sake of science," he added, grinning wickedly.

"Well," she said, wrapping her arms around his neck and pulling his mouth down to meet hers, "since you put it that way, I'm willing to donate my body . . ."

The kiss she gave him was wild and warm, wonderfully loving. Jack was only too happy to return it.

Several hours later they were cradled in each other's arms, discussing what a success the experiment had been. In fact, Jack was blown away to realize that their physical reactions had been even stronger this time, now that their emotions had been exposed. The feelings showed no signs of fading.

Love wasn't a four-letter word any longer. It was an aphrodisiac more powerful than any perfume could possibly be.

Ed cried when he explained how fulfilled he felt. She cried again when he took her in his arms and fulfilled her right back.

Jack carefully kissed her tears away, reminding both of them that their passion was here to stay. With a lifetime of love ahead of them, he figured it was time for a new mission statement. A new rule to live by. One that would last them forever.

A happy ending is the best kind of all.

THE EDITORS' CORNER

What do you get when you pit the forces of nature against the forces of man? You'll have a chance to find out after reading the four fantastic LOVE-SWEPTs coming your way next month. Two couples face the evil forces in their fellow man while the other two do battle with nature in the form of a snowstorm and a hurricane. The result is four mind-blowing romances that'll leaving you cheering—or crying—at the end!

Loveswept favorite Charlotte Hughes dazzles us with **JUST MARRIED . . . AGAIN,** LOVE-SWEPT #902. Ordered by the family doctor to take time off, Michael Kelly decides to spend Thanksgiving in his mountain cabin, away from the pressures of work. Maddie Kelly wants to spend the holiday in *her* mountain cabin, away from her well-meaning family and friends. Unfortunately, it's the same cabin. Since their separation nearly a year earlier, Maddie and Michael have been avoiding each other. When a sudden case of amnesia and a snowstorm trap them in the mountains, together with two dogs and a stowaway nephew, the couple have no choice but to endure each other's company. As they get to know each other and the unhappy people they've become, they slowly realize that what tore them apart the first time around could be the very thing that binds them together. Charlotte is at her all-time best in this touching novel of love rediscovered.

In the land of **SMOKE AND MIRRORS,** Laura Taylor paves the way for two lost souls in LOVE-SWEPT #903. Anxious to begin a new life, Bailey Kincaid fled from Hollyweird with divorce papers in hand. As co-owner and president of Kincaid Drilling, she's responsible for the safety of her men, and she's determined to make the person who is sabotaging her job site pay. When Patrick Sutton found himself interested in the shy wife of one of his clients, he immediately distanced himself from her. He's stunned to find out the woman who captured his attention years ago is now the strong-willed woman in charge of the construction on his property. Patrick had taught her how it felt to ache for something she could never have, and it hadn't been easy to get him out of her system. He insists that they were never strangers and that they deserve to follow where their hearts seem determined to lead. But can the sorrow that haunted their nights finally be put to rest? Laura Taylor writes a memorable story of fated lovers who discover the great gift of second chances.

In **ONLY YESTERDAY,** LOVESWEPT #904, Peggy Webb teases us with a timeless romance that knows no bounds. A sense of *knowing*, a sense of belonging, and a sense of love have kept Ann Debeau in Fairhope, Alabama. When she haggles with Colt Butler over a charming clock, she's pleasantly surprised at the attraction she feels for the handsome stranger. Sorting through her grandmother's belongings in the attic, Ann Debeau finds a stack of love letters addressed to a man she's never heard of. A hurricane strands her there with the waters swirling ever higher, and Colt comes to her rescue, only to be stuck right alongside her. As they read the letters, a mysterious force whisks them in time to a place where both have been before and into a relationship that was never consummated. In the past, Colt and Ann find a ghost that demands closure and an enduring love that refuses to give up on forever. Peggy Webb challenges us to believe in destiny and reincarnation, in this jewel of a Loveswept.

And in **LOVING LINDSEY**, LOVESWEPT #905, Pat Van Wie introduces neighboring ranchers and one-time best friends Lindsey Baker and Will Claxton. Years ago, a misunderstanding drove Will from Willowbend, Wyoming, but he's always known that one day he would return to the land he loves best. Never one to desert a lady in need, he offers Lindsey help in sorting out the trouble at her ranch. Though he swears he's looking to buy his land back from her fair and square, Lindsey's sure that Will is the one responsible for the "accidents." When one night of promises in the moonlight leads to more than just kisses, the dueling ranchers realize they're not just fighting for her land. In the end, will the face of her betrayer belong to the man she's dreamed of for so long . . . or the man she's trusted for all of her life? Pat Van Wie proves once more that those we love first are so often those we love forever.

Happy reading!

With warmest wishes,

Susann Brailey *Joy Abella*

Susann Brailey   Joy Abella
Senior Editor   Administrative Editor